Praise

In Other Lifetimes
All I've Lost
Comes Back to Me

"Sender matches the light topic of youthful lost love with the extreme heft of the Holocaust . . . and comes up with a miraculous balance between the personal and the universal."

— Ann Patchett, author of *The Dutch House*

"Wholly original, lyrical, fierce, these stories confound expectations at every turn. Courtney Sender writes about passion and loneliness, faith and longing, heaven and hell with a clear eye and a compassionate wit. This collection expands and celebrates, even as it sometimes upends, what it means to tell a love story."

— Alice McDermott, author of *The Ninth Hour*

"Courtney Sender's stories are fierce and tender, exploring the urgency of desire, the restlessness of longing, and the way that both trauma and the will to survive can be a haunting inheritance. Sender moves gracefully between the surreal and the everyday, capturing the way romantic love can be at once impossibly strange and mercifully familiar."

— Danielle Evans, author of *The Office of Historical Corrections*

"Trust is the soul of these stories, and it flows both ways: the trust Courtney Sender has in her reader and the trust the reader feels deeply and truly in the hands of such a generous, intelligent, offbeat, singular writer. These stories, structured in an utterly original way, are rare and real; they get under your skin."

—Elisa Albert, author of *Human Blues*

"Reading these stories is like hearing a series of songs you love— the rhythm, the feeling, the physicality, the words. Literary rock 'n' roll."

—Aimee Bender, author of *The Butterfly Lampshade*

In Other Lifetimes All I've Lost Comes Back to Me

STORIES

COURTNEY SENDER

WEST VIRGINIA UNIVERSITY PRESS

MORGANTOWN

Epigraph from Elena Ferrante, *Those Who Leave and Those Who Stay*, trans. Ann Goldstein © 2014 Europa Editions. Used by permission. Epigraph from Kate Leland, "Eating Ortolans," *New Literature Review* © 2020 Kate Leland. Used by permission. Epigraph to "Lilith in God's Hands" from the Holy Bible, New International Version, NIV. Copyright © 1973, 1978, 1984, 2011 by Biblica, Inc. Used by permission of Zondervan. All rights reserved worldwide.

Grateful acknowledgment is made to the following publications, where these works originally appeared: "In Other Lifetimes All I've Lost Comes Back to Me" in the *Adroit Journal*; "Black Harness" and "For Somebody So Scared" in the *Kenyon Review*; "Only Things We Say" (as "These Words I Unlearned") in *Louisiana Literature*; "Epistles" in *Cease, Cows*; "An Angel on Stilts" in *AGNI*; "The Docent" in *Witness*; "I Am Going to Lose Everything I Have Ever Loved" with Graywolf Press online; "Lilith in God's Hands" in *Shenandoah*; "To Do with the Body" in *Prairie Schooner*; and "A New Story" in *Jabberwock Review*.

ISBN 978-1-952271-78-6 (paperback) / 978-1-952271-79-3 (ebook)

Library of Congress Control Number: 2022948273

Book and cover design by Than Saffel / WVU Press

Maybe, in the face of abandonment, we are all the same; maybe not even a very orderly mind can endure the discovery of not being loved.

—Elena Ferrante

*Love, it's not that we were wicked,
some things are just too good
for the eyes of God.*

—Kate Leland

CONTENTS

....

In Other Lifetimes All I've Lost
   Comes Back To Me 1
Black Harness 13
For Somebody So Scared 21
Only Things We Say 47
Epistles 63
An Angel on Stilts 65
The Docent 79
I Am Going to Lose Everything
   I Have Ever Loved 91
Lilith in God's Hands 119
To Lose Everything I Have
   Ever Loved 129
To Do With the Body 151
From Somebody So Scared 165
Missives 187
A New Story 193

Acknowledgments 203

IN OTHER LIFETIMES ALL I'VE LOST COMES BACK TO ME

....

Yes, all of them.

B the drunk and C the poet and D the coward, and smaller stories too, minor loves, Y the Capricorn and X the sock salesman and W the scholar and V the painter, they all come back and I am the biggest regret of their lives. I was the love of their life that they let get away. Anywhere from thirty-eight to eighteen years ago.

In the meantime they had families. They had wives, they had children, they had furniture they bought and dogs they raised and soccer teams they coached.

In the meantime I waited. I sat here in my wooden house in my wooden chair and I looked out my wood-framed window at the wooden swing hanging from the tree in my front yard, and I thought: *Please. One of you, any one of you, change your mind and turn around and please come back to me.*

My loves, I will give anything.

Anything, I used to think. I would have given up my arm, my house, my heating. I would have groveled at their feet or tithed to their church. I would have had no sex or sex every hour, I would have fought off armies, I would have lost my name, if one of them had come back in time for the life I'd wanted—which was simple, and unambitious, and looked like my parents' lives. A life where somebody cooks dinner for somebody else. A life where, if no one buys groceries, it's some kind of failure. A life where, if your train's delayed, it's someone's job to pick you up. A life where someone's flying cross-country, and your stomach never settles until they're on the ground again. A life where you're praying the whole time they're in the air. A life where you think, If you come home to me again then I will thank my God and bless those wings and love, I will give anything.

Just one of them. I'd been willing to become the woman I would have been with any of the seven: different women all, and all different from who I became, which is a woman unformed, staring out a window, watching my swing rot year by year. With B I'd have become playful, with C quiet, with D unstoppered; with Y edgy, X poor, W snobbish, with V addicted. Each of them had their perks and their downfalls. With D and W I'd have lived in a house we owned in the suburbs, with a finished basement and two cars we drove and one that just sat in the driveway; with X and C and V I'd have lived in a city apartment complex that was half public housing; with B and Y I'd have traveled, I'd have rented, I'd have been always going somewhere new.

For twenty years I was ready. I would have lived any of those lives. I would have packed my bags or planted gardens. I would have straddled their waist or been tied to their bedpost. I would have frozen in Boston or burned in Boca. I would have gone camping in the woods or skiing by a chateau. I would have cooked every meal or put takeout on speed dial.

In all worlds I'd have stayed Jewish, and a daughter, and a granddaughter. I'd have sung showtunes in the car and in the shower. That's it. Those were the only constants I required to remain identifiably myself.

They never came. I lived in a rented one-story house on the far edge of a city, I traveled rarely and for one day at a time, I waited. And waited. My heart became harder; my life became smaller. I looked out that window hopeful every morning. I looked out that window hopeless every night. And sometimes I grimaced, and sometimes I doubled over, and one day I noticed that I never went outside. Out the window was a porch and a set of stairs that no one climbed, and beyond that a swing on a stretch of grass that ended in a fence I couldn't see. My singing sounded strange to my own ears.

And now: here they are, at last, at my doorstep. Now:

"Here we are," they say. "You are our great missed chance. We didn't know it, but we've missed you all our lives. Somewhere in the pit of us we have been always screaming."

Several, seeing me, wipe tears. They are old now, they are bald in ways I anticipated and ways I didn't, in aggregate I love them more than it is possible to love, I want to check all their foreheads for fever. The ones I'd expect to be holding flowers are holding flowers; the ones I'd expect to be empty-handed are empty-handed; D of course has an atlas wrapped in newspaper, V a small canvas he painted. In aggregate they are my most intimate body of knowledge.

Yet the longer I stare at them, filling my stairway, the more in aggregate I am sadder than it is possible to be sad—because if only from this gray-headed mass a single one had peeled off like a rogue grape from a cluster, then my whole life would have been set. I'd have been a person too, like them, instead of a stiffening wasting window-gazer. I'd have loved them. Each one, for different reasons and in different ways. For X and Y I would have learned Spanish, for C Hebrew, for B Urdu, for V art history and for D war history and for W history of western thought. With C and D I'd have had laughing kids who loved their grandparents, with B and X kids who hated them, with W kids who looked down on them. With V and Y, no children. B and C and V would have protected me in alleyways, B with an arm around my shoulder, C always half a step ahead, V with a knife in his pocket. X and W and Y I'd have protected. D, whom I'd loved best—for him I would have killed.

Do you understand, I want to ask them, *what it is to wait?*

But I know they don't. They have been busy. They have had wives to buy groceries for and children to put onto airplanes and airplanes to will safely across continents. They have lived in cities and countries and Boston and Boca and places I never thought to imagine, probably, Chile and Nigeria and the town where I grew up.

I do not let them in. I open the window and lean out. The wooden frame is hard in the flesh of my stomach.

"Well," I say, "which of you is it?"

They murmur to themselves. A bouquet gets dropped and picked up again.

"It's all of us," says B.

"All of you."

"All of us or none," he clarifies.

He had always been the one to set the rules the way he wanted.

I think of what it would be to have all of them. How we would fit in my bed. The sex had been different with each one: with B clumsy, C formal, X slow, Y absent, V sweet, W rough. With D alone it felt like making love.

"And how," I call, "would you expect to get along?"

Murmuring, again. Such bafflement before me, on the part of my boys. My men. I look into the throng of them on my porch. In all these years I've tried to fill in what has happened to them. B and Y had office lives already fully formed, clear pathed; C and D were strivers—the artists were strivers of course, their lives hard to picture—but so was V the painter and so in his way was X the salesman;

W the scholar got by on little ambition, seemed likely to go further than the others anyway because he was handsomer, somewhere within himself he was sure of this. I try to verify. Who looks shabby, who looks neat; who looks healthy, who looks sick. They all look low, dissatisfied. On every face a look of hunger.

"We would get along," says B, "in honor of you."

"Of missing you," says C.

"Of loving you," says D.

Then yes, say the words in my heart. *Come in. What are you waiting for?*

"And how would you repent?" I say.

They each left me for their different reasons. Y never felt attracted to me, C felt too attracted to me, W had a girlfriend, D had a wife, B lived far away, V was busy and X wasn't ready. *Maybe,* they all said, to the last. *Maybe someday.*

So I waited. In order not to hate them, I remembered: D was my best friend. C was my best conversation partner. Y was best looking, X the best listener, B was smartest, W kindest, V was saddest. In order to be able to say yes when they came back, I forgot: the look of their backs in retreat. The sound of the car doors closing. The precise way each one said the word *goodbye.*

They move toward my front door.

"My loves," I say. "I have to think."

They'd each have hurt me in their different ways. B never would have compromised, with him I could have cheered on Messi's millionth goal and still if I asked him to the theater he would have said it's boring, baby, go alone; with C, if I wanted a purple quilt for our bedroom but my in-laws wanted yellow, I'd have slept in marigold duvets until I died; with D I would never have had him completely, he would go away to airports and bat his eyelashes and miss his flights and girls like I was would fall in love like I did and he would not say no. With Y there would have been comments sometimes, about the uncalloused smoothness of my palms or that I always fed the parking meter; with V I would have known every detail of his high school girlfriend, I could have spotted her in the middle of Times Square, her face would show up endlessly in his portraits; with X I'd have watched him watching how large a slice of cake I cut for my plate; with W, even on vacations we had saved for, he would have taken from his briefcase yet another paper he just had to read tonight.

Still. Even still. Even knowing what I know, I've lived my whole life waiting for a single one to look behind him and say, *Oops*.

They rattle my doorknob. They strain the bolt. It's clear they believe I'm still human. I'd thought so too, with my everyday waiting, but now in the face of them all I understand I've become something else. I try to tell them: Do you know what so much unused hoping does to you? It drives you crazy. It burrows into your heart and rots you like a piece of wood. Or else it ages you like a carburetor ages. You hiss and spark except when you are cold.

Yes, say the words in my heart. *Come in. What are you waiting for?*

"Go away," say the words in my mouth. "Go home."

"We have pulled down our homes for you," they say. "We've left our wives. We've wrecked our lives. You want us to come back. We're here."

"So come back thirty-eight to eighteen years ago," I say. "Not now."

Within my heart I have welcomed them in. I have taken their coats, I have found enough vases and enough chairs and enough cups for the water or wine or coffee or tea or soda or beer or whiskey each will want, I have let them pet me, I have let them cry, I have found a way to stack them widthwise so they fit on my mattress, I have kissed B's forehead and D's lips and C's neck and Y's chest and X's navel and W's hip and V's thigh. Within my heart I've woken up.

Outside my heart, I say: "If you can swing me on that swing then yes."

They turn around. They look at the scene I have been watching through the window from the time I was twenty, then thirty, then forty and up and up. The green grass. The wooden swing. The fence beyond that I can't see.

"But wait," says W, "the swing is gone."

It's true the wood gave way a decade earlier.

"But wait," says X, "where is the tree?"

It's true the great oak fell last spring.

"But wait," says Y, "where is the rope?"

There was a flood. Three years ago, or thirty.

"Didn't one of you bring rope?" I say. "Aren't any of you trees?"

"Maybe we can make a swing," says V.

I let them look around. I let them see the nothing I have seen. I say, "From what?"

....

The minor loves go seeking. But the major loves stay on.

B, C, D: the smartest, the oldest, the dearest. They knew me best; they hurt me worst.

"You were afraid of heights," says B.

"You didn't like to swing," says C.

"You never wanted to go to the park," says D.

"Of course I wanted to," I tell them all. "Of course I did."

....

The minor loves return. They haven't found anything. My rules are firm: they have to go. I watch them. I relearn what I've made myself forget, so I could say yes to them on an impossible longed-for day exactly like this one. The look of their backs. The sound of the car doors closing. The precise way each one says the word *goodbye*.

I settle into my seat by the window. I am comfortable here. I will go back to the task of forgetting. I will go back to missing them forever, forever wishing please. One of you, any one of you, change your mind and turn around and please come back to me. Forever thinking love, I will give anything.

It's V who comes back.

V a minor love, the painter with whom I would have been an addict, the saddest. The one, therefore, I might have loved the best, with time. He'd been a little schmaltzy. He'd held my hand across tables, studied my knuckles like they reminded him of some sea-thing tossed out in a bottle years ago, pressed his lips to the knob at the back of my wrist. He'd been the most recent, the last. He is striding toward my front porch, holding his little canvas under his arm.

"Listen," I say, "I'm sorry, I can't make an exception, what will the others—"

He doesn't climb the stairs. He walks up to the window, leans inside, and pulls me out.

He is not gentle about it. His canvas falls, facedown, on the back are pencil sketches of heads that look like mine. I get a splinter in my side. He doesn't seem to care. I have not touched any of my loves today, major or minor; to touch him is a furnace.

He has me in a fireman's hold. I twist my neck and see the revelation on his face.

"You can tell," I murmur. "I'm not human anymore."

He nods.

"You've turned to wood," he says.

It's D who comes back next, and with him I am afraid to touch, I pull away, I press myself into V's shoulder, I can't help it. But my majorest love puts a hand on my hand and with a dead man's reflex I hold back.

Each of them takes a piece of me. They turn me face-up

in their arms. V and X support my knees, Y and W my hips, B and C my shoulder blades. D cradles my head in both hands, like an egg. I am held, I am touched, I can feel each one like a lover in our bed. They start to rock me. Slowly at first. Back and forth and back they rock. I watch their faces, I see each one as he'd have been as a father over a bassinet. They move out to my extremities. Y and W take me by the ankles, B and C by the wrists, they are men swinging a grandchild at the playground, they are swinging harder now, higher and higher, their faces are blurry, sick and old, I can't tell whether they intend to let me go or rock me—please—just one short second longer.

BLACK HARNESS

....

There are so many boys.

There are so many boys that Olivia can barely remember all of them. She writes their names on a list. Sometimes forgetting even one seems like defiling something sacred, but other times she knows that what she does with these boys isn't sacred. Times like those, she pictures each boy in the world, a tiny piece of bad-luck broken glass. She has an empty-vacuum heart. She feels oppressed by the sheer number of boys: not Gus, not Gus, not Gus, not Gus.

Gus and not. The only two people she knows.

....

Ten years ago, Gus and Olivia had delighted in their mutual blond-haired, blue-eyedness. They were nineteen. Whenever strangers asked if they were siblings, they laughed, telling Hitler down in hell, "You hear that?"

The week in Berlin was their first, giddy trip together. They slept, clothed, on a shared twin mattress beneath a plantless potted plant-hook. On their first morning in the hostel, sunlight streamed across their faces in bed. "Blinds," Gus moaned, pulling her on top of him. "Guten morgen!" Olivia answered. She kissed him on the eyelid. She went to the window, laughing at Gus, who was overdramatically covering his head with his arm to make her laugh. The window was the size of a door, the street outside was alive with people, Olivia could smell meat already roasting. She hoisted herself into the frame. She put one leg outside—and almost stepped on a long trail of broken glass shattered on the sidewalk.

She wrenched her socked foot back into the room.

For a long minute, Olivia stared at the shards sparkling between the cobblestones. She heard Berliners wishing one another *Guten Morgen* in voices much more guttural than her own.

"Beer bottles, Liv," Gus said finally, joining her at the window. He shaded his eyes with his hand. "Only beer bottles."

....

In Berlin, they learned by the light of the splintered Pilsner, everything was double. History breathed on these sidewalks, holding up a broken mirror.

Olivia no longer wanted to do a pub crawl. She registered them for their hostel's tour of Sachsenhausen. History lite: the camp had held political prisoners, not Jews. Gus's ancestors hadn't guarded there. Olivia's hadn't died there.

Their tour guide was one of two on the train, new and nervous, wearing a blue shirt. As the un-air-conditioned cabin sighed through the countryside, Olivia laid her head on Gus's sweat-damp shoulder.

"There would have been fields," Gus said. "I never realized."

And Olivia nodded and loved him, because she had been gazing out the window with the same thought. There would have been fields beyond the wooden tracks that carried her Nana's brother and sister away. There would have been sunshine. The pastures then would have sprawled as widely as these now, the fences would have been as wooden, the flowers as brightly yellow.

"It wasn't black and white," Gus said.

"Sometimes it looked like this," Olivia agreed. She kissed him on the cheek, to say she didn't blame him. "Sometimes it looked beautiful."

....

But as they approached the camp, the landscape changed. Maybe their mindsight grew stronger than their eyesight. Maybe history held up a stronger lens. The fields browned. Squat houses appeared, rusting cars in their driveways. The bones in Gus's shoulder dug into Olivia's temple.

When at last the train stopped, Olivia disembarked with relief and turned left, following the tour group in green. "Blue shirts, Miss," her own guide called. "To the right."

Olivia glanced at Gus. His face looked pained, but hers

must have looked panicked, because he said, "Let's go home."

In later years, writing her long list of names to keep track of, she would wish she had.

....

Backyards with swing sets abutted the camp. As Olivia watched, a shirtless child lifted her baby brother into a black harness swing. Their tour guide counted his disembarking passengers, index finger pointing at each human person stepping to the dirt, *eins, zwei, drei*. He consulted his list of names. Counted again. "Is Yoni Levy here?" he called, experimentally. His consonants were brusque.

"Right here."

"And Rosa Levy?"

"Got her," said Yoni. "Maybe you could keep her."

Gus tittered. Rosa elbowed Yoni in the ribs.

"It's all right, love," said Gus, squeezing Olivia's shoulder.

"Augustus Muller?"

Gus said, "Here."

The guide looked a lot like Olivia and Gus: blond, with nimble fingers and blue eyes under glasses. But, Olivia decided, the guide looked a lot more like Gus than like her. He was tall, with angular cheekbones and a flat nose. His blond hair was straight as a nightstick.

"Gus," Olivia said. She took a nervous half step forward, then back again. "Don't let him call my name."

She felt light-headed. She felt the plastic walls of the

twenty-first century melting all around her. Here were the barracks; here were the bunks. Here was the man, calling names.

"Olivia," Gus said.

"That's not funny."

"Olivia."

"Stop it."

"You've got something on your . . ."

Gus tapped her on the tailbone.

Certain parts of each other's bodies Gus and Olivia knew, deeply and intimately: the mouth; the eyes; the scalp, nose, neck, hands, knees, ankles, feet. The rest they were saving for later, after they married. This had been Gus's idea, but it suited Olivia; she had spent the weekends of her life at home with her brother and parents, she was a young nineteen. She hadn't known a sex drive before Gus, and she liked the one that was shaping itself in his image.

"You've got," Gus whispered. He drew two loud breaths. "Blood."

Now that Olivia was thinking about it, she could discern a warm, soaking feeling between her thighs. With the flight and the time change, she must have miscalculated when her period was due.

Olivia shivered, despite the heat. Her Nana had had one brother and one sister, both lost by war's end. Neither had been here, in this camp. Their blood had spilled elsewhere, distant places, Poland and Croatia.

But now here she stood. She hated Germany, for needing

her this way. How much of her blood would this land have to drink before it was sated?

"You're right, Gus," she said. "Let's go home."

She meant America.

"Derek Parker?" said their guide.

To Olivia's surprise, Gus shook his head. "Clean up first," he said. "Then we'll go."

There was embarrassment in his directive, a lack of practice in alluding to her body's mechanics. But there was something else, too. Though they had spoken of it rarely, Olivia knew that Gus was ashamed of his grandparents. He worked to keep his voice soft, because theirs had been hard. But his orders to Olivia now sounded firm, and unyielding.

"Final call," said the guide.

Olivia's heart thrashed in her throat. Gus pulled her toward him. He unzipped his saddlebag, took out a crumpled windbreaker, and knotted its sleeves around her waist. What he didn't do was run back to the train with her. He didn't clap his hands over the guide's lips.

The guide said, "Olivia Wasserman?"

Olivia said nothing. She felt the sad beginnings of a shift, some empty-vacuum space left over where love has shrunk to pity. Gus didn't see: bloodletting was in her genes, as surely as her blond hair. It was hers and her brother's and their parents', it was her cousin's, sideways and up along their lineage. Her Nana's lost brother and sister—there were so many lost, their names on the wrong lists, their bodies spattered open as a consequence—had understood blood.

Who could say whether they'd wanted to understand. They had become it.

"Olivia Wasserman?" The guide's voice contained relief: he had identified his missing person; he was a fine leader, worthy of this first responsibility.

"Say you're here," said Gus.

Olivia felt the need to repudiate Gus. Maybe later she would regret it, or forget it, or want Gus back or get him back or blur this fight with endless others in their history, but for now: if he wanted her to cover up, then she would mark her place in blood. If he wanted her to wait, she'd sleep with every person willing. If he wanted her to be counted—

Olivia untied the sleeves at her hips and swatted Gus's jacket to the ground.

The sun reflected yellow on the refurbished barbed wire atop the camp's fence. As Olivia boarded a train by herself, the little boy next door tipped sideways and slipped from his black seat on the swing, and his sister covered her ears when he started to wail.

FOR SOMEBODY
SO SCARED

. . . .

"Say no to me," she said, and I hesitated but did it.

She seemed to get off under me.

"No," I said again.

"I dare you, Bridget," she said. "I fucking dare you."

"No," I said, enjoying myself this time. "No, no, no."

Afterward she explained that she's learned, if she asks for her rejection, it doesn't hurt nearly as much.

"Damn," I said, "you are breaking my heart."

She turned her face into the pillowcase and laughed at me. "At first when you say you're in heartbreak, you think you're referring to pain," she said. "After a few years of it you learn it's actually about function. Your heart breaks the way a toaster breaks. It just doesn't work anymore."

She thought for a while. The sun stroked a long finger down her cheek between two slats in the blinds.

"You can press all the buttons, but ain't nobody getting any warmer."

. . . .

This worried me, of course, because she was the first girl I'd ever slept with, and I hadn't had the years of long-term lone-liness that seemed to be the only experience she respected in another human being. I was a girls' girl who'd never ex-pected to become a girl's girl. Then Kaye showed up with her short hair and smart suit and oxfords, and she kind of confused me, and by the time I knew what was where I was tracing the crescent moon tattooed across her chest like it was a holy site. Within a month I'd memorized the particu-lar curvature of her every rib, yet I was never sure I was get-ting her warm.

Of course she accused me of willfully not knowing what I was doing. According to her I was halfway out the door even when I was sleeping in the crook of her arm, because it was clear I wasn't really a lesbian so what the hell was I doing hauling out to her cabin in the middle of the woods every evening, pretending I intended to keep slapping around with her. I told her who says I'm out the door, who says it's clear to anyone but her, I intended to talk and cook and laugh with her for the rest of my days until I died.

"Ah," she said, from her back. She wore the knowing look she often got when I exposed my membership among the too-well-loved. "But do you want to fuck me?"

"I want to do that and I want to do better than that," I said.

"There is nothing better than that, Bridget," she

answered, every time. Then she curled up like a pill bug and shoved herself into the crack between the wall and the mattress, so I had to reach out an arm if I wanted to be sure she was still in the bed. What she was saying was absurd; she was the most creative and sharp and surprising person I have ever met, and there was so much beyond her body to worship.

I loved her body, too. I swear I did. I can recreate it with the slope of my tongue alone. It has been twelve years. I miss her so much I wonder if I've broken in the function-way she talked about. Something cold inside me where there used to be a will to fire.

This is the story of the night I left her.

....

When we met, she was living in a cabin in the woods in Vermont, surrounded by her pen and ink and pencil—which was a blessing. If she'd worked in oils we would have died of fumes. She was not outdoorsy; I at least liked biking the path toward her house, but she barely opened the windows, and even then she hated if birdsong set the tune of her dreams. Her dad came up from Boston every Sunday to drop off groceries and take care of maintenance and reset the rat traps around the porch. I taught her to unclog her own shower drain because I felt, for a grown woman, it was embarrassing.

I don't know what I was doing in that town. I'd been living in Boston, half-dating a nervous professor type who ended up skipping town. The night he left, the long-haired guy on the barstool beside mine paid for my drinks; the next morning he said let's do this again soon, and the next month I followed him north. Even while caressing his hand over the gearshift, I didn't much care about him. Or rather, I thought he was worth trying to care about, but I kept on failing. He was the sommelier in the wine cellar on our town's narrow Broadway. I worked the front desk at the art gallery next door. Kaye walked in one morning in August and stood there in her suit, arms crossed, studying this post-card-sized collage in the corner that no one had noticed before. It was all red tissue paper. Saturated, veined.

"Are you the artist?" she asked me.

"No."

She looked me up and down. She looked back at the piece.

"You could be," she said, the way people sometimes say you could be a Claire or an Emily. Then she talked me into the most freewheeling conversation I'd ever had, about politics and war and art, and how the fact that we can talk about politics and war and art in public but not love and sex and heartbreak was fundamentally sexist. I thought she might be part artist and part woman, but wasn't sure where she landed on either. Then abruptly she said, "I don't want that piece."

"Okay," I said.

"I said I don't want it."

"I heard you." I was noticing the black point of a tattoo

just visible above the top button of her collar. I was wondering if I would be able to keep having a conversation with this creature, or if I would need to install her in the back of the gallery first, to get used to her out the corner of my eye.

"I might come back tomorrow," she said. She paused until my gaze moved up to hers. "But just because I'm lonely."

I laughed, I was so shocked. She didn't come back tomorrow, which she later told me had been a monumental effort of will. When she wanted, she wanted hard. I spent the whole day waiting for her, polishing the glass over the print she liked. I kept the store open an extra, unpaid hour hoping she would come. Later she told me that my waiting had been by design. She wanted me to think I could lose her—because she was no good at restraint once she loved somebody, and she loved rarely but with brutal force, and she always knew instantly if she could be in love with someone, and the distance between knowing she could be and being was a vibrating string she didn't see the end of, and once I had her there would be no risk of losing her, which would make her so dispensable that I would leave. But that first day. So early on, she could still muster restraint.

"You could have just come back," I told her, after we'd been together a couple of weeks. But I have never been the truth addict she was. I don't consider it some moral virtue to express my personal suffering or psychoemotional tricks. I've always thought there were good reasons to keep these things private. So I never told her how over the course of that second day—hour by hour staring at the door, blowing the slightest dust off the collage, refusing to go to the bathroom in case I missed her—I realized by her absence that I already depended more on her presence than on the sweet wine pourer whom I met three times a week next door. If she'd come in that day, who knows. Maybe she's right. Maybe I would have found it too strange to want the sort-of woman with the smooth, slim jawline. Too easily satiated, I might not have had time to develop in hunger.

She did the right thing, that first day. She left me hungry.

. . . .

She never told me what the hell had happened, why would such an air-condition nut with allergies to bees and apples and a serious aversion to most mammals, cats excepted, move to the woods at the age of thirty-four to be supported by her father. She would have told me, if I'd asked. But over the course of the autumn we spent together, I learned to conserve my questions. She was unable to answer with anything but total honesty, and by the time I started suspecting I would leave, I had the sense that each additional fact I learned about her loneliness was another sin I would commit against her.

Still, I have my guesses. She was an extroverted artist, itself a contradiction, energetic and stylish and born for the city. But every daily urban slight that was imperceptible or insignificant to me was a rejection that wounded her. She would say to me, The mean clerk rang you up with a discount; The butcher didn't have to give me the butt; I thought she'd have asked for my number. In a city, the sheer number of people who could not-want her in the sheer number of ways she hoped to be wanted would have defeated her at every turn.

Or maybe it was simpler than that. Occasionally, obliquely, she referred to a short fling she'd had before me that didn't matter anyway. But I think that old rejection may have tipped her over, and she never stood back up again. Her father made a comment to me once over Sunday breakfast: "You should have known her before."

"Before what?" I said, and he looked at me like if I didn't know, then I didn't deserve her.

She wasn't really supported by her father, I should say this. Financially I mean. Looking back, he probably paid the maintenance fees for all the security he'd put in for her—hidden alarms and wire traps and surge-protected floor outlets, he loved her, he wanted her to be happy even if it meant snaring her inside a cage. But her art actually made money. This was a shock to me. I worked in the little gallery, named Gallery, and knew there was no money to be made in art. We swung a profit by selling chocolate to the locals and umbrellas to the tourists, and overcharging for wine and cheese nights, and trying to stagger our hours against the hours of Wineglorious next door. Once I started dating her, Gallery also received an anonymous monthly donation of $1,000, so I guess I should note that her dad was supporting more than just her. He'd been a somewhat famous architect when she was young. The style of his buildings was clean-lined and lean, and was called April, which had been her mother's favorite time of year.

Her father had designed the cabin where I loved her. It was one big room, cut in the middle by a spiral stairway to a sun-drenched reading loft with triangular windows and a view of the topmost cone of the steeple in town. She used the loft as a studio. When she was feeling playful, she would send me up there alone and have me do ever more tragic renditions of Juliet. She would die in a hundred thousand ways trying to reach me.

I was a kind of artist too, nominally. She thought I was the better one of us, a misjudgment I know she believed. She had no platitudes in her: if she thought I was bad, she would tell me. Once I published a poem in *Poetry*, and she walked to town and bought fifteen copies and had me sign them and gave ten to her dad and kept five around the cabin, and still she had the nerve to say, "It's your biggest publication but it's not your best." Which hurt me, though I didn't tell her. The next week I had a different piece come out in a little nothing online zine, to no notice whatsoever, and she read it and put her hand to her heart and said, "There you go."

She put her hand to her heart and said that's where I go. I wonder sometimes if I'm in there still.

....

Two days after her first visit to the gallery, she came back.

When I saw her I was so relieved. I'd spent the night at my boyfriend's apartment above the wine cellar, unenthusiastically stroking his beard, pushing his hand off my waist saying I was too hot, thinking of the black point of the tattoo I'd seen above her collar. What was the rest of it? I dreamed it was a ship's bow. I woke thinking it was a fisherman's hook. It was always the sea, with her, and us so landlocked. I opened Gallery that morning in dread that I would never know.

At eight after eleven, she walked in. "You like collage," I said, as soon as the door chimed. I'm sure I flushed. I hadn't even given her the time to look at something and prove it.

She didn't appear to mind my gaffe. If anything, she seemed pleased. She said she was an artist; I asked what she made. It was a simple set-up. She said, "Come over tonight and see." That was what we both wanted, and I think we both knew, so she left without pretending to consider buying.

That first night, I biked as far as I could through the woods to her cabin. Then I latched my bike to a tree and walked the narrow dirt path the rest of the way. I was lugging a backpack that held the little collage she'd admired and a bottle of Cabernet I'd ridden to the next town over to buy. I was too nervous to be afraid of wolves. The door to her screened-in porch was unlocked; I knocked; I heard sizzling, something metal colliding with something glass. She couldn't hear me. I let myself in.

The single room was bright from yellow track lights on

a high ceiling, and wallpapered in words. Pen-and-ink calligraphy in black frames. She was wearing a lacey apron over
a trim suit and pouring eggs into a pan at the stove. When
she heard me, she turned around and kissed me in the
middle of flipping an omelet. She was not one for restraint.
I unbuttoned her shirt as I did my boyfriend's, and learned
the tattoo was a moon, a black crescent belly-up above her
heart. I touched it and kissed it—I don't know, in later years
she has accused me in my head of being too afraid to kiss
her skin directly and so fetishizing this part of her that
wasn't her. But every time I fight back, no, I loved the moon
that night because it was doubly her, flesh and artistry right
on top of each other, a thrilling sacred abundance of her.
That was the night she told me to say no. "No," I said, and
so began the season of my life that was more yes than I
would ever know again.

In the morning, the stove was still lit and the whole place
smelled of burnt egg. She woke and saw me wake and her
eyes creased downward when she smiled. "You were good,"
she said, and laughed, "for somebody so scared. Stay for
breakfast."

I was so overawed that I was afraid if I stayed another
second I would give myself away. I kissed her on the cheek
and said I had church. As soon as the door closed behind
me, I realized that I was still carrying the collage in my
backpack, and that I wanted to keep it; it reminded me of
her.

The path from her screened-in front porch meandered

for a mile and let out at the parking lot behind Gallery. I walked back replaying one kiss in particular she'd given me, on the inside of my elbow, a place I couldn't remember ever having been kissed despite having been kissed in seemingly infinite combinations before. I tripped on more than one tree branch. The way she'd dipped her head from my breast to my arm. The sway in her neck. I ran right into a man heading down the path. Plowed into his chest and before I even looked up I knew it was her father. Something the same in the heart. His daughter's tongue was still strong in my imagination; I was embarrassed, but he wasn't. He was a big guy, a young mid-sixties, copper bearded, still wearing his wedding ring though her mother had died years before. I wasn't sure if he knew his daughter was a lesbian, then I thought just look at her, then I wasn't sure if he was okay with her sleeping around, then I thought she's thirty-four, you mute, look up and say something.

He was holding a wicker picnic basket covered in a napkin. He took in my disheveled ponytail. "She didn't ask you to stay for breakfast?" he said.

"She did." I wasn't sure if I should add, *Sir.* "I didn't want to impose."

He clicked his tongue. "Stay."

We walked back to the cabin together. We passed my bike latched to a tree, which I had forgotten completely. Inside, I dumped my backpack under the record player at the foot of her bed. Her dad opened a window against the charred smell. He set out fresh cream and blackberries, which he'd picked on the way. "Look at those thumbs," she laughed at him, "stained purple like a kidney." Like a heart, I thought, like the inside of her throat, like the inside of her thighs. It turned out he came from Boston every Sunday to bring her breakfast and a record from his collection. We all ate berries on toast and sang along to some Stones and stayed until it was dark. When he left, I did not go with him.

"I'm never leaving," I said, all bluffing bravado, as the sapphire sky darkened to black.

"Is that a promise?"

Instantly, I shut up.

She said, "What you mean is you'll stay until you stop wanting to."

She breathed in my ear. I pawed at her chest. She pushed me to the bed. I thought: It's too early to tell you I could love you.

She said: "I have loved you since yesterday."

....

I was mad at her dad for a long time. I still am. He had loved her and her mother so much and so well that to be unloved was worse than foreign to her. It was inhuman. She could not reconcile the experience of being deemed losable with the experience of being human. Her dad's brand of endless devotion—that's how steadfastly I'd sworn I would love her.

"I didn't tell you I would love you that way," I told her the night all this was leading to, the night I left. She was sobbing, as I'd known she would be; I was prepared to stay until she had exhausted herself, until she noticed that her own arguments were running in circles. I was prepared to be that generous and no more. "I never promised that."

"You made me feel like you promised it, though," she said. "That's the same, that's the fucking same."

I exploited her, that night. She was right but I didn't tell her. I let her hear her own reasoning and believe that the il-logic of the words was truer than the fact of the feeling.

That was the thing about her: she was so very easy to leave. In the end, she seemed to demand it. The more she looked for why her loves had fled, and made art of her un-flinching findings, and wanted hard and answered honestly, the more impossible she made it to stay, even though she remains the single most exquisite being I have ever kissed. I have prayed under the little steeple that some angel far better than me finds her and loves her and kills me with jealousy.

The point is, I argue with her in my mind at night, that I am married to a man now who has the look of someone longed for and not someone longing. He picks up when his brother calls and simply says, "Hello." He doesn't answer my "What do you want for dinner?" with *Whatever you want,* or *An ex of mine once left me over salmon,* or a med-itation made up on the spot called 'Meditation on Want-ing' or 'From Whence Predilection,' or *Your poem on Eden needs a line where Eve displaces Lilith.* He says, "Chicken, not the wings." And I am able to grant him this thing he wants, and he doesn't tell me with his voice—or worse, his eyes—that his needs are ever-growing and complex and that I will never answer them all, even as I am the only thing he wants, closer, closer.

Yes, of course: I know that just because he doesn't say it doesn't mean it isn't true.

....

The art she made was pen-and-ink calligraphy of other people's words. She stroked each line onto parchment paper without being asked, then rolled up the sheet and mailed it in a tube to the unsuspecting author, with a self-addressed envelope for optional donations. Those few who didn't want the pieces sent them back, and these she framed and hung like wallpaper around her cabin. But I was shocked by how often the recipients donated. At first I said, "Well go find Warren Buffet's PO box," and she said, "I tried that but it didn't work, billionaires don't pay for anything."

Instead she sent her artwork to the locals who wrote into the town paper. "I find the lines that are poetry," she explained one Saturday in September, slicing a jalapeño for a stew.

She loved cooking. She always insisted that she hated cooking actually, she just loved doing it for me, alone she lived on cereal and popcorn, but then she'd go and peel potatoes with such slow tenderness that I would get bored. That day, I read the work framed on her walls. *I didn't tell you anything / depends upon your answer / but alas*, read the page above the foot of the bed. *To elect one thing is maybe / to pass up another,* read the one at the top of the stairs. *You teach yourself / not to be tentative*, read my favorite, right beside the oven. I asked her about that one. "Retired food writer," she said. "Some reader asked a question on pot roast. How does a person know how much to salt?"

We were eating that night on the money from her first commission, which she'd accepted on the condition that she wouldn't do fluff about dead dogs or grandmothers. She knew how to pick the phrases that were worthy of art; other people didn't. "We don't see ourselves," she told me. Then she reconsidered. "I see myself," she said. "That's why people think I'm ugly. It's why they leave me."

I made a show of ogling her breasts.

"Different kind of ugliness," she said.

"I can handle it."

She shook her head. "You don't understand," she said. "Yet I have told you plainly how it is."

"That's D. H. Lawrence," I said.

This was one of my best joys, impressing her. I was so fascinated by her mind, and my favorite high was when she approved of mine.

She salted a tomato. I kissed the low part of her back where the apron tied, untentatively. She raised an eyebrow. I pulled her from the oven. She laughed. "What brought out the beast?" she said.

It was useless to say that the slope of her back against the black prerogatives of trees outside had seized me suddenly;

she'd already called such images a form of pretty platitude and one she could not stand, one so egregious in fact that it made her love me less, which was impossible, and besides I could praise her body but was not a real admirer of the form. So I said, "That you're the poet, really."

It was true. She remade my brain. She gave me images through which I cannot help but organize the world. I hate this sometimes, and sometimes I am terrified of losing them. This orange slice, I'll sometimes think, this bit of nail I've clipped, this curl of blood in the toilet bowl: they're never lima beans or cups or archways. They are always crescent moons.

I bit her thigh through her jeans. "The original writers make the food," she said, because she liked to play the game of talking until she couldn't. "Their words. I just arrange them pretty on the plate." She paused to breathe. I accomplished this so rarely, giving her what she wanted the way she wanted it, shutting off the mind that I preferred on. Then she said, "If the writers are satiated, it is with themselves," and I stopped and looked up and said how could anybody ever lose you, and she laughed or moaned and said just wait.

....

That was when I was trying to learn how to fuck her, which was all she wanted and all she wanted me to call it. Sex was the thing I was worst at and the thing we did most. She was not one for restraint; she viewed conversation as preamble and she liked the main event. When I told her how much I

loved her mind or her talent, she was offended. She wanted
to be loved for her body. She wanted me to feast on her
without civility, leap onto her and bite the back of her neck
in the middle of the night, join her always in the shower.
She was never not hungry.

I was not the best at this. My boyfriends had been eager
as they were taught boys should be, and with them I'd been
reticent as I was taught girls should be. They had respected
my rebuffs; the professor, it seemed to me, had even been
grateful not to have to work up the energy. So I had grown
used to being the one saying stop.

"The less-hungry one," she told me early one Sunday in
November, when I expressed a preference for sleep over sex.
"The less-hungry one holds all the power."

Yet she held all the power. She wanted sex, she got it. She
wanted fresh syrup and a Hendrix record, her dad walked
them over. That morning, my sommelier showed up behind
him.

"How could you," he accused me, pointing wildly at her.

I shrugged. Her dad said he'd thought the guy was a friend
of ours; he gave him a strawberry and said, "You'd better go."
The boy shouted for another few minutes and went.

But his visit did some terrible work on her. She opened
the door he'd walked out of, just to slam it again. "That,"
she said, banging a pan on the burner. "I've wished someone would regret me like that, but I'm always the one who
shows up at the doorsteps."

Her dad said, "Bridget's right here." He looked at her

with so much sadness. He said, "Bridget has not left your doorstep."

Apparently I was unsatisfactory. She wanted me to be everyone before me, too. She pulled a cigarette from a pack I'd never seen under the sink, and smoked it at the table. She said her heart weighed a hundred pounds, possibly she was having an aneurism. She said unless she'd been the first to love me, then to be with me would always mean that there was someone somewhere, longing.

When she went to the bathroom, her dad made her excuses. "She's had a hard time," he told me. "Too much bad luck." I stabbed a pancake with my fork. "I don't pretend she's easy to handle, Bridget," he said. Then he paused for too long, until I looked up, with the feeling that he was grabbing me by the eye. "But she will love you like no one else."

"I know," I said.

We heard something thud in the bathroom. He sighed. "You should have known her before."

Her dad left early that day, before we could sing along to the Hendrix that he'd retrieved on hands and knees from the back of his attic. She didn't kick him out; he seemed simply unable to watch her in this kind of furor. She stood on the front porch staring after him long past the point when he had disappeared from sight. I joined her out there.

"The worst thing in the world," she said, "is knowing that my dad knows I'm not happy."

I opted not to show my offense, though for the second time that day she had dismissed me.

"Can't you fake it for him?" I said. "Maybe then at least—"

She snorted. "I don't love him that much."

I remember that moment. The leaves beyond her had gone brown, the short hairs on the back of her neck were bristling, she had an unlit cigarette between her fingers, she was obviously shivering but wouldn't admit it. It was the first time I wanted to tell her yes, it's true, laying yourself so unforgivingly bare is ugly. Maybe it's noble but it makes you ugly. Cover up those parts, I wanted to tell her. Yes, that bareness was why she was a better poet than I was. She would always be better and I wasn't jealous.

Within the hour, she calmed down. She came inside and put on a sweater. She called her father to thank him for the record. She seemed to regret what she had said about him; she tried to justify it in a hundred ways. She said, "He's the one who taught me to be honest." She said, "He knows me too well to believe me if I lied." She said, "Faking anything would erode our relationship."

I tried and failed to kiss her that night. *I'm not happy,* I could hear her saying, even as her body fell asleep enclosed by my body.

I would not say I was the less-hungry one, K. You lay there washed in moonlight. I dreamed of solving your tattoo. It is just as easy to die of starvation silently as screaming.

I have never, not once, gone knocking at her door.

....

"Aren't you ever satisfied?" I asked her one night, near the end. She had slipped her hand between my legs at five in the morning, and outside it was freezing, almost Christmas, and I would have to walk a mile through the ice to open Gallery by sunrise.

She said, "Do you know, if you sleep six hours one night, you need to sleep ten the next to make up for it?"

I believed it. I was exhausted. When I needed rest this badly, my old boyfriends had allowed me blocks of sleep that were a half-day long.

She said, "The body remembers every hour when it didn't have enough."

....

And yet our last fight was not about my reticence with the vagina. It was about loneliness. She was cleaning the New Year's confetti off the kitchen counter and all of a sudden she said, "What did you do with the body."

I thought she was talking about the sommelier. Only an hour ago we'd been joking about the day he showed up at the cabin; we'd done an operatic reenactment on the balcony. I said, "I buried it out back, why, the smell bothering you?"

She said, "You have never asked me that."

I said what, when should I have asked, what are you talk-ing about, but it was the rare moment when she seemed to stop herself, shake her head, rerack the steak knives, decide some things were better left unsaid.

She was in a strange mood. She'd been getting the kitchen prepped to do a soufflé. I told her I didn't feel like cooking and she took it personally. "You mean you don't feel like cooking with me," she said.

I let this pass. My willingness to entertain her bad psychologizing was, I'd gathered, the key feature I had in common with her exes. I never said no, it's not true just because you can imagine it is. Whatever skewed nutjob thing she wanted to allege was okay by me. That she alone was unable to love someone she could leave; that all promises were platitudes; that the concept of losing with grace was just another way to say shut up. I never said no unless she told me to.

I defrosted a frozen pizza for dinner that night. She took her half upstairs, to her studio, while I ate at the table. Still, I didn't know our little scuffle in the kitchen had been a fight until hours later, when she woke up and woke me up and the real moon glowed on the crescent symbol over her heart. She told me she'd wanted to send me home tonight after dinner. I had hurt her, she said, normal people would have asked me to leave, but then she'd have been left alone and she would rather sleep with even me than no one.

"You slept by yourself for ten years before me," I said. And then I said, "Oh," and I knew this was the moment I should have asked, *And all those years the body, what did you do with that?*

I didn't ask. Even me, she'd said. As if I were a disappointment or capitulation. A tree branch slapped the window above her hip. I heard a lump of snow fall from the ledge. Finally she said, "Until you know loneliness that has no end, you will never be able to love me the way I can love you."

"I'm sorry that you have been lonely," I said.

She snorted. She turned back to the wall. The heating vent was directly under her side of the bed, blowing madly; she was shirtless, though I wasn't. I studied the little knobs of her spine. If only she had let herself fall asleep. Done herself this favor. But despite what she would say about her great capacity to love, her fidelity to her own emotions was the strongest loyalty she had. Soon enough she said, "Until then, never"—and I believe today that she was wishing on me all the years of loneliness that she had suffered.

The fact is that I have never spent more than a few months single. I have mourned her and I miss her, but it's been the same since as before. I don't know what it is that makes love so hard to come by for some people and so easy for others. I'm nothing very special, but men and sometimes women, they want to know me, and once they do they want to stick around. Even while I was with her, the sommelier was willing. The girl behind the deli counter blushed when I tipped two dollars instead of one, and the son of our only real buyer asked me about watercolor while pointing to an acrylic. I married him, later. He worked as an occupational therapist and had no opinion on poetry and our courtship was short.

Being a disappointment, by the way: it doesn't make a person feel good.

That night, the knobs of her spine elongated in front of me. I watched her curl into herself, make herself small and ready to attack. She was refusing to let the moment pass. I wondered if the culprit was our playacting on the balcony; if she was still angry a month later that the sommelier had shown up fighting for me and no one had shown up for her.

She said, "You still didn't ask."

I was too tired to want to know. I thought of ways I could avoid a fight.

"I have a gift for you," I said.

I went to my backpack, which had been sitting under the record player since the first night I'd come walking back with my bottle of Cab. I unzipped the front pocket. And there it was: the little collage. Red tissue paper, saturated, veined. I wanted to kiss the glass across its face; it was like looking back at her, strong and strange the day we'd met.

I walked back to the bed. The room was dark, and cold in patches, hottest by the headboard. I held the collage out to her and turned on the lamp above her nightstand. The corner of the picture frame touched the moon on her chest.

"I told you I didn't want it," she said. She leaned forward, so the frame dug into her skin. "You think I want everything?" she said. "You think I'm incapable of not-wanting?"

I told her to take the thing. I told her she was trying to pick a fight. I told her I couldn't see why. I told her it was a present from our first night together. "I am trying to love you," I said.

She said, "You are doing it wrong."

I thrust the collage into her hands, but she wouldn't take it; I let go and she didn't grab it and it fell to the floor. The glass shattered. Shards splayed from the nightstand all the way across the kitchen floor.

To this day I have never been angrier. I said I was leaving. I meant for the night. But she started sobbing like I'd said much more than that, like it was the end of the road and forever, and this act of hers is what first suggested to me that it might be.

She said, "I knew this would happen. You couldn't even last the winter."

She made me do it. She'd been daring me from the moment I met her to leave her. How long until a person takes the bet.

"You promised me an every-single-Sunday love," she said.

She meant a love like her father's. That kind of forever.

I looked around at the staircase, the oven, the shards on the floor, and for the first time I saw the truth of what she'd dragged me into, and was horrified: she'd made this place a temple to her own rejection. The artworks she framed were the pieces that had been sent back, the ones that had said no. She'd given away all those hundreds who said yes.

I thought I might vomit. She was sure I would hate her, she'd made herself hateable. She had committed this debasement on this beautiful woman, the one I'd first seen with that smart suit and slim jaw in my gallery, the one with a moon above her heart, this woman I loved she had torn her to bits.

"I didn't tell you I would love you that way," I told her, knowing it would kill her. "I never promised that."

It took all night, the night I left. It turned into morning. She shook with sobs. She accused me of not crying. My leaving took on an inevitability that I couldn't have stopped if I'd wanted to; she'd have had to stop it. She'd have had to say, Okay, I'm sorry, I recognize you aren't leaving me, I can take a shower and open the window and buy bread as if you aren't leaving me. But she couldn't. She said, "You're leaving, you want to leave"; and when I fought back she said, "You're lying"; and when I didn't fight she said, "You see?"; and she worked so intently to convince me that in the end she succeeded. Fine, I didn't even see how much I didn't want her. Fine, I didn't love her as much as she loved me. Fine, I never could.

Do you understand now, K? Have you kept forcing more women who love you to admit they don't, even as their hearts are falling to their feet inside them?

K: What if I told you it has been twelve years, and I still try to solve your tattoo.

The morning I left, I ran into her father on the path to her cabin. He looked at me and I might have been doing anything, going out to pick berries for breakfast, but the betrayal must have been there in my face. I said, "Sir," but he waved one hand and I saw where his daughter got her ferocity, I shut the fuck up. He was a giant, almost seventy and in excellent shape, broad shoulders, big wide thumbs. He was holding a picnic basket the size of a small cat. It was coated in a doily, faded off-white lace. He said, "You're not hungry for breakfast, Bridget?"

We stared at each other for a long time. A bird trilled something jarring in the distance. Inside my gloves my fingers were burning with cold. My stomach growled.

He said, "I don't forgive you."

Sometimes when I think of her, it's his forgiveness I find myself craving, not hers. I think of him standing in the road, massive, bringing her a picnic of fresh cream and berries. I think of him very old now and stooped over and still walking that long road holding a wicker basket draped in lace. I think of him putting on a record, hoping she'll sing. I think of him singing. I don't know why.

ONLY THINGS WE SAY

....

My son joined the Marines. His neck grew thick and his shoulders widened, and he took off for Japan.

I'm proud of you, son: I couldn't speak the hackneyed line of other fathers, dropping their babies at boot camp. I wasn't proud. My pride in Theo could never be his killing arm or plate-smooth head.

"You don't have to go," my wife, Mel, told him.

Even under his olive hat, Theo was able to roll his eyes. He was able, but he chose not to. He looked straight at Mel, his brows slanted toward his nose. "Yes," he said, "I do."

Our daughter, twelve years old and still holding my hand, nuzzled into Theo's side. Our second son grabbed the top of her head like a basketball in his huge hand.

"Nicholas," said Mel, warningly.

"Screw you, Nickle," said Cat.

"Caitlyn!" said Mel.

Now Theo really did roll his eyes, thank God. And there I found it, my pride: his easy roll-off-the-shoulders. So unlike mine or Mel's. That morning, before Mel woke, I'd shut myself in our bedroom closet and read my file folder of Theo's report cards. There was my other pride. Theo hadn't gotten into Yale this year, his dream school, but he'd accepted Rutgers and could transfer. He was planning to transfer. Theo had never picked up a free weight in his life. He hated every sport I'd ever convinced him to try, from baseball to tennis to hide-and-seek. He hated track. He hated swimming. He liked chess.

....

We Skyped with Theo in Japan.

"What's it like over there," I said, enduring the pause where another father might add, *my boy*.

"Good," he said. "Easy," and he laughed. I wondered if the laugh concealed humiliation. I wondered if the other boys had made him drop his vocabulary like a too-heavy textbook. I imagined him, my toothpick of a son, five six at a stretch, raising a rifle and watching the muzzle fall beneath the target, unable to hold it in place. I pictured the other boys—huge boys, football players—catching him by the back of the neck and tossing him into a wall. Cackling at him. I'd had to see the principal about fighting twice before Theo hit high school, four times about bullying. I'd had to threaten to sue. I would have, too. I would have sued.

"Really?" said Nickle. "Easy?"

"Sure," said Theo. His cheek was still smooth, unstubbled. "I mean, if you think blind obedience is mindless enough."

I couldn't tell if this was sarcasm.

"Cat joined Pascack Democrats," I said.

Mel pinched me on the thigh, where Theo couldn't see through the grainy screen.

"Yeah, Cat?" said Theo. He'd always loved his little sister. This had been a saving grace for our family, since Theo had been opposed to Nickle from the moment I tossed the boy a ball and he caught it.

"Yeah," said Cat. "We're protesting the war."

I smiled. Cat had ended up the most like me; she even looked like me, God help her. She *cared* about the world, she really did. I'd never expected Nickle to take much interest in life beyond our local high school, and even Theo for all his brilliance knew the world as he found it in books. Cat was the only one who . . . when I gave her a window, she looked out.

"Shoot," said Mel, "honey, I think you're breaking up."

"Protesting, Cat?" said Theo.

"Darn. We'll call you right back."

"The picture's fine, Mom," said Cat, but Mel had already ended the call. Theo's face snapped away. My hand floated up to the screen, palm curled sideways to catch him back.

. . . .

Nickle came home from a Giants game with a *Support Our Troops* bumper sticker. Mel joined a Military Moms support group. "Look," she said to me, opening a briefcase stuffed with legal documents and old Italian takeout receipts. From between the pages of a red-penned contract, she tossed a photo onto our bed. A group of boys, spines straight, hands behind their backs, heads shaven, camo-clad. Did green even camouflage a person in Japan? In Iraq or Afghanistan? Or was the uniform a stylist's holdover from Vietnam, a man my age unable to design new patterns for new war.

I turned the photo upside-down.

"Try to love them," said my wife, flipping the photo again. There on my pillow: two dozen closed-lipped eighteen-year-olds. Killers. "They are all Theo."

"Thank God we've got two spares, huh?"

Mel did not laugh. She did not agree. She looked at the image as though it really was Theo, cutting his middle school lips through braces against his trumpet.

"How do you have time for these groups?" I said, nudging her briefcase with the tip of my sock.

She tugged at a thin strand of hair. Mel had had curls, when we met. Thick ribbons of red hair that caught in my mouth when we kissed and my nose when we slept. Since turning forty, her hair had gone flat.

"How do you pretend you don't?" she said.

When I was younger, when I was first married, I had this ridiculous notion that a wife stood beside you through life's storms. The fact is, marriage is a rope around your waist, tied to a woman across the sea: you'll drown if she goes down, but there's not much you can do to stop her.

. . . .

Theo decided not to come home on his leave. He stayed in Japan, growing wider by the day, doing God knew what with God knew who for God knew which reasons. Cat set up a blood drive through Nickle's sophomore-year basketball team, then his baseball team. I bought pumpkins from the supermarket, then watermelons. In May, Theo changed his Facebook picture: Happy Mother's Day, Mom. A photo of Theo as a toddler, snuggled on Mel's chest, half-gnawed pretzel sticks in a line of peanut butter down her blouse. I'd taken the photo. Nickle had been strapped into a baby harness around my shoulders, Cat a lima bean in Mel that we hadn't yet discovered.

When Nickle showed us the Facebook photo over Mel's breakfast in bed, she smiled for the first time in months. I said, "Who put him up to that?"

"Can't you let her have a little peace, Dad?" said Nickle.

"Since when does your brother go sentimental over Mother's Day?"

"Maybe he's changed," said Cat, and this fact was so obvious it broke my heart.

....

During Nickle's junior year, he Skyped with Theo more and finished his homework even less. I was afraid he'd fail out; I started doing his homework for him, but staying up all night relearning trigonometry got Mel's attention, and she made me stop. It wasn't fair, she told me. To the other kids in class.

"I'm not going to college," Nickle informed me one morning in March, when I set down an SAT prep book.

"Don't worry, bud," I said. "You'll get in somewhere."

"No," he said. "I won't."

"Your grades slipped a little this semester, sure, but Coach won't let you rot."

Nickle shook his head. He was a good kid, but always worried. He'd gotten that from me. I remember being his age, staying up nights, legs shaking under my covers, sure my number would get called. Making plans to be in Montreal before my first friend could get drafted. Looking up midnight train schedules. My dad must've hated to see me that way. Layers and layers of fathers hating to see their sons with fluttering nerves.

"It's not Coach," said Nickle. He looked straight at me, and his steady gaze didn't seem worried at all. "I joined the Marines."

....

"You are killing your mother," I said. I did not say, *You are killing me.*

....

"You're an idiot," was Cat's assessment of her brother over dinner.

"That would make Theo an idiot," said Nickle.

"Then Theo's an idiot. Do you have any idea what you'll be doing over there?"

"Do you?"

She chewed in silence. None of us knew. Freedom, terror, tyranny. Blood, uniforms, target training. All just words.

....

On the sunny Saturday morning when we were getting ready to drop my second son at boot camp, the doorbell rang. "Hi, Mr. Cohen," said the girl on the porch. "You must be very proud."

I shook my head. "Are you?"

I'd always thought of Nickle's girlfriend as a joke of a prom date, bobble-boobed, the type of cheerleader a boy like Nickle felt obliged to date for a few years before he found someone more like his mother. I expected her to say *Yes*, or even *No,* or maybe *Maybe.* What she said was, "I never thought I'd be a military girlfriend." She paused. "It's selfish, huh? I'm scared for Nick, I really am, but more I'm scared it changes me."

I wanted to hug her. I wanted to tell Nickle, *Nick! You found a good one. I didn't think you did, but you did.*

Instead, I camped out in the kitchen making turkey sandwiches for the road and listening as they said goodbye. My son's girlfriend said, "We'll be together for a long time, won't we?" and my seventeen-year-old said, "Yes, forever"— but these are only things we say to ease the pain of missing each other until we can unlearn the impulse.

"You're eavesdropping," said Mel, laying a hand on my shoulder.

I gave her a Ziploc bag full of food. "You see him off," I said. "I can't."

"You have to." Her hair was falling out in patches. Her eyes around the irises were more gray than white. "What if he . . ."

He won't, I didn't say. *He'd deserve it,* I didn't say, because what if God heard?

I didn't go to drop him off. My big lanky basketball player, six feet four inches tall, thin as a windowpane, suited up for war. Loping out of the house into his mother's car, not a glance at the basketball hoop I'd nailed to a tree when he was only eight and part of the town rec league. Theo had hated sports, and Cat had wanted to be a ballerina. And little Nickle-in-the-Middle had joined a team.

After Mel's car pulled out, I got into my car to join them. How could I let my Nickle go, what if I never saw him again?

But traffic was heavy on the highway. An accident: two guardrails and a semi. Once it was clear I'd missed my chance to say goodbye, I turned the car around and never told the girls I'd tried. Cat slept on the floor of Nickle's room that night, curled on the circular rug beside his bed. I'd always hoped she loved him, but hadn't known for sure.

. . . .

Theo renewed his contract. Nickle shipped out to Afghanistan. Mel became treasurer of Military Moms. She and I took Cat to church.

Secretly, I spent my Friday nights at temple, while Mel stayed late at work and Cat at student government meetings. Nickle had always been the one of us with religious feeling. He was the one reaching to set the angel atop the Christmas tree, the one bowing his head, taking his hat in his hands, performing the sign of the cross before his games. Theo had enjoyed his mother's faith academically, but the boy possessed as close to no spiritual feeling as a person could get. Cat hooked onto the charity piece of church, and the youth group, and the way the songs could lift her up; she liked Latin, she said, more than English; she hated thinking of any of the five of us in heaven. It was the only time I'd seen her worry like Nickle: she was a little girl with Mel's curls, yanking at them in the backseat after Sunday School. She'd learned about the afterlife, she said. She feared that heaven was a fuller place than New York City, and that it would take eternities for us to find each other there.

Heaven, I told her, had an excellent subway system.

Cat might have been Jewish, in another life. Maybe that was my mistake. Maybe I'd given up too easily. Maybe if I'd fought, decades ago when Mel and I got married in her parents' church, I could have stopped all this. Mel had bent over backward for the husband before me, then stood up again, convinced it was a man's turn now to bend to her. So I'd bent. Looking back, of course, I could have argued. I could have raised my sons under a God who'd had none. I could have kept them.

....

In her senior year, Cat ran for class president. Mel helped her make the signs—Caitlyn for Change, Go In on Cohen—and tied her hair into a severe knot for campaign speech day.

"They're my fault," I said into Mel's hair that night. "The boys. I stayed at home. They never had a male role model."

I could sense Mel agreeing. "It's not your fault," she said.

"I thought, at worst, it'd turn them gay."

Mel said, "That's not funny."

"You think I should have stayed on Wall Street, don't you?"

"I don't think anything."

I laughed at her, a mean laugh. Her patchy hair was gray at the roots.

"Fine," Mel said. "Plenty of Wall Street dads have kids who join the Marines, okay? Plenty of construction workers' kids join the Marines. You have no effect on what they do."

"You don't believe that."

"Stop torturing me." This she whispered. She sat up, swung her legs over the side of the bed. "Be a man for once, Simon," she said. "It doesn't matter what I believe."

I felt myself boiling. I caught her by the shoulders. I pushed her to stand up, wrapped one arm around her breastbone from behind, found the high waist of her underwear and pulled it down her thighs. The white cotton fell to the carpet. She stepped out of it. I pushed her forward, stood behind her, shoved her face-first into the closet door.

"Cat'll hear," she said.

I imagined Theo's report cards in their folders in the closet, rattling. When we were finished, I cried. I reached for my wife's hand, to turn her around, to kiss her, but Mel was already headed for the shower. She shook out her shoulders. She said, "I needed that."

....

After school, I waited in the kitchen for the front-door latch to come undone. "How were the elections?" I asked, when my daughter appeared in the doorway.

"I got president."

"Way to go, Chief!" I said. "I thought you would. I'll get your celebration dinner moving."

I raised my hand for a high five. Cat smiled and high-fived me back. "And I joined the Marines."

"Very funny."

She laughed, then headed upstairs to her room. I put water on to boil and a chicken in the sink to defrost. The phone rang.

"Hi, Mr. Cohen, this is Caity's science teacher, Douglas Freeman."

I was breaking lettuce for a salad. I remember the snap.

"I'm just calling to see how Caity's taking it. It was a close race."

"I think she's pretty happy, Doug."

"That's a relief. We didn't see her the rest of the day, we thought she . . ." He cleared his throat. "I told her life is easier without that responsibility."

The lettuce fell onto the chicken's thigh. I hung up. I felt my heartbeat in my ears.

"Cat?" I said. I don't remember moving, but I was outside her bedroom door. I studied the faded stickers on the knob. Before she was born, Theo and Nickle had decorated in anticipation of her. They had gotten along that day. Then they had used marker to track her growing-up, until she got sick of waiting and stood on a chair and Sharpied a line where the wall met the ceiling.

"You got president, honey?"

I tried the handle. Unlocked. Cat had never locked her door. That was Theo, needing privacy for no good reason; and Nickle, worrying when he had his girlfriend over. We hadn't heard from the girlfriend in a year by then. I had liked her.

I found Cat at her desk chair, crying. My Caitlyn never cried. None of my children cried, Mel didn't cry. I was the only one who cried.

"No," she said, "I lost." She said some other words, but I couldn't understand them. "I signed up for the Marines."

What was left of my heart fell away. Cat was compact and sprightly, but she could never hack it as a soldier. She could never shoot a gun. She couldn't find the will. "Why?" I said, struggling to keep the judgment from my voice.

She shrugged. My articulate Cat, nearly class president, so full of ideas and ideals, she only shrugged.

"Because you miss your brothers? Because you want to fight?"

"No," she said. "I don't want to fight. I hate the war."

"Then why help it?"

"You know what the recruiter said when I told him I wanted to join? He said, 'We need people like you.'"

"Honey," I said. "Caitlyn. I need people like you."

"The Pascack Democrats don't."

"The Pascack Democrats are a bunch of know-nothing eighteen-year-olds."

"Yeah, well, so am I."

....

Cat went away with the rest of them. Mel and I attended church, and temple, and support groups for military families. We learned vocabulary I'd never wanted to learn. KIA. MCT. Assaultmen. Artillery cannoneers. If I had gone to Vietnam, if I had learned this language rather than my kids, could I have warned them away from it?

How are you, son? I learned to say. *Thank you for your service, Private. Write your mother, Corporal.*

I miss you. How could you? Please come home now. That's enough.

These words I unlearned.

....

Six years, three children, one empty house, and Theo sent an email. He was coming home at last. He'd gotten into college. Yale.

I ordered Italian takeout, to celebrate.

"Penne vodka!" Mel reminded me in the shower, lathering shampoo into my hair. I tossed a handful of suds in her direction, careful to avoid her eyes. She laughed. She kissed me with a soapy mouth.

The doorbell rang. I volunteered to answer, realizing I had ordered marinara, worrying about how I would make up my mistake. I wrapped a towel around my waist and threw on a white undershirt I found at the top of the hamper. There were yellow stains under the armpits.

I unlocked the door, hoping the delivery guy would be an asshole, so I wouldn't feel so bad about blaming him for the mistaken sauce.

The delivery guy was tall and wide, and he was wearing a United States Marine Corps uniform. His hat was in his hands.

"No," I said.

"I'm sorry to disturb you, sir."

"No," I said, and I worry that, in front of this stalwart soldier, I began to cry. This must have been how Theo felt in high school, wanting to be braver than he was, thinking he might train himself into courage, read enough books about strength to become strong. Jesus God whoever you are, don't let it be Theo. Theo is too gentle. Theo is done already, done with all this, his term ended years ago. He's coming home. He's going to college. It was all a mistake, Theo as a soldier. The wrong dot penciled on a test. I spent a lifetime protecting Theo, my firstborn, my runt, my little filled-out full-grown favorite. You can spend a few short years.

A black-clad man stood beside the Marine, wearing a long vestment. "In the course of service," said the Marine.

"No," I said. I covered my ears. Nickle. My tall worried saint of a Nicholas, my point guard, the son I painted signs for, cheered for, tore my throat shouting across the finish line. Fifteen years I used up hunching over Nickle, helping him with homework. I didn't say goodbye to Nickle. I didn't hug him around the waist, as high as I could reach. Nickle gave his faith to you, whatever you is up there, Nickle put his whole self in your hands, he is guileless, he is scared, you wouldn't crush him.

"Sir," he said, and this enormous alive soldier reached out to hold my hand, and it was something in the quietness of the gesture, the lack of buck-up-and-be-proud, man, and I knew. Cat. My baby Cat, my Pascack Democrat.

"Don't tell me," I said. "That's an order," I said.

"Honey?" called Mel.

"Finding change!"

I stepped backward into my home, back toward my wife and my file folders of our children. I shut the door, but the arm of the Marine reached out and blocked the jamb. Doorknob in hand, I stared at that wide wrist, those fingernails cut to stubble. I could have crushed his whole fist. I could have fought. I could have lifted a handgun, a rifle, a bomb, a grenade. I could have done anything, really. I could have aimed. I swear, I could have killed.

EPISTLES

....

I don't have a soul mate. When I turned fourteen, God Himself delivered a letter telling me so. "I'm sorry," God wrote, "I forgot to make one for you. Accept this token of my apology." And He proffered the letter and let me keep it, and it was signed The Lord God so I decided that I would, and not to sell it on eBay, though it might have paid off the school play.

But I met a boy tonight after rehearsal, a beautiful boy with a midwestern voice and brown hair soft as latte foam, and now I have my suspicions. "God," I said to the ceiling, "did You intend Your letter for a different Isaac someplace else?"

I waited a month but didn't hear from Him, and in the meantime the boy was heating me licorice tea before my ballads, so "God," I said, "about that letter—did my mother put You up to it?"

I wanted to wait a week, but I only lasted three days

before the boy pledged he'd become a better stagehand—wear black darker, pick up couches quicker—in time for my debut. "God," I asked the sky, "won't You please fix Your mistake?"

I waited until opening night. The boy was applying my eyeliner with careful strokes, and when he brushed a stray eyelash from my cheek I showed him God's letter, palm-sweaty and fist-wrinkled. I watched him read it in the mirror. He frowned.

"God," he said to me, and I closed my eyes, sure my mascara would run, "how many copies of these things d'you think the guy hands out?" And I watched him pull a wrinkled letter from his pocket, and he took my face in his hands as the pages fluttered to the floor, and he drew my eyes in spirals of kohl until the curtains peeled aside.

AN ANGEL ON STILTS

....

Once I met an angel on stilts.

She was standing next to the seesaw in the park, her neck in the clouds. It was the first day of spring. She wore long jeans under her wings and a T-shirt with an elastic hem. She and her stilts were the gray of old white shoes.

She made me think of you. I remember you so well, my friend, so tall, so ready to swoop in and save me from behind the scenes and then pretend you didn't, that you don't even exist, the way angels do. You used to call your friends and have them waiting at the taxi stand when I got too cold in the Baltimore winter and caught a southbound train to a city I didn't know. You'd buy an air mattress and have the delivery girl deliver it, and set up the pillows, when some guy you thought I shouldn't sleep with asked if I had a guest bed. You'd drop a twenty in my mailbox when there were dinners you weren't there to take me out to.

You're dead now, or just gone. One's no different than the other; to the unloved, the beloved must become dead.

She who is friends with the man who didn't love her either never really loved him or loves him still.

I love you still, my friend. I have been looking for you for eleven years.

So when I saw the angel on stilts, her head up in the clouds, I said, "How small does the world look to you from up there?"

Her wingtips hung a yard above the treetops. She pinched her forefinger and thumb a quarter-inch apart, to show how small my head seemed. She pinched the whole park to the span of two inches.

She was operating at a different scale than you and me. I was thrilled. I asked her could she see you someplace down here, and I described you, but you are eleven years older now and who knows how much more sad.

Because I couldn't see her eyes while she did me the favor of searching, I decided she was you, a bit. I decide this about people sometimes, when I'm missing you the most.

She couldn't find you. I said it was okay, that you'd left a while ago and forgotten where I lived was all. When I'm missing you the most, this is the story I let myself believe.

Because I'd decided she was you a bit, I asked her, "Would you kiss me?"

You see, you never did.

She said she hasn't kissed anybody since her little baby daughter, and besides she's not a real angel: these legs are just long stilts; these wings are papier-mâché and glitter.

She wears this getup because that daughter of hers died, but before then, boy did the girl love it when they played dress-up in the park, and now she has nobody to play dress-up for.

I hugged her around the stilt, knowing she couldn't feel me. The seesaw tottered. The world is so full of real sadness. Sometimes I am mad at you, because you only invented mine. You could have just loved me back the way I wanted, and then I wouldn't have to carry a good-as-dead man like a stone on my back the way this woman carries wings.

"I love your dress-up," I told the angel on stilts. "Those feathers! That height!"

"Truly?" she asked me. From the tone of her voice, I thought she smiled.

"Truly," I said.

But I lied, a bit. I miss you. Sometimes it feels like there is nothing true to say, except those words.

. . . .

Once, before you went away, I met a real angel. He was sitting in the first-floor window ledge of a bookstore, typing on his laptop. This was January eleven years ago, when I was young and a little bit beautiful and living next door to you. I had just taught my class this little fable, "Angel Levine," which had been taught to me as magic, but had since grown too outdated to be anything but history. I was walking past the bookstore deciding I would never teach that story again.

The angel on the window ledge said, "Wow, it's you!"

I was cold and didn't know him. I ignored his call.

The angel on the window ledge said, "I wrote a poem about you!"

I raised my scarf over my mouth and said nothing. You and I both knew to ignore people who sang songs or painted pictures or told fortunes. Once, an astronomer in coattails on our street corner had told us if we paid a dollar we could look through his telescope and see Mars. I had wanted to see Mars but didn't want to pay a dollar. We kept on walking to the laundromat. Then on the way back home, the astronomer gave a little bow and said, "Okay, for her it's free." I looked at you wondering if you'd slipped him a dollar, but you looked away, like you always did when I tried to pin your kindness on you. So I peered through the telescope at a piece of black construction paper pasted to the aperture, a little red circle Sharpied in the middle of a Wite-Out sky.

Afterward, you laughed and clapped and insisted I'd really seen Mars.

The angel on the window ledge said, "Years ago."

"What?" I said, stopping in front of him—even though I didn't want to stop, because back then whenever I was going home, I was going home to you.

"I wrote a poem about you years ago," said the angel on the window ledge.

The thing is, he didn't look like an angel—not like my angel on stilts. He looked like a middle-aged man who was a month or so away from being homeless. But the other thing is, and this was why I stopped, that the story I'd just taught, "Angel Levine," which I have not taught since, is about an angel who appears to a Jewish guy who doesn't believe. And the Jewish guy is wrong not to believe, of course.

"Here," he said, and turned the laptop around on his knee so I could see the screen. "I'll prove it."

And he showed me this website of his, which had an outdated rounded-font look to it and a clear pub date of five years earlier, on which he'd posted a sonnet titled "Jewish Girl Full of Hope," about a girl who had just taught "Angel Levine" and was walking down the street in the cold when she stopped to talk to an angel on a bookstore window ledge about this man who loved her but would never tell her.

"Never tell her?" I said. I pulled my scarf up tight around my nose. I didn't like this prophecy, which made me want more than anything not to believe it.

"Well," he said, "unless . . ." And he clicked down the webpage, just under "Jewish Girl Full of Hope," to another title: "Neighbor Boy Waking Up."

My heart stuttered. I reached out, scrolled down, but the angel on the window ledge pulled the laptop away. "For him," he said.

I sprinted the eight blocks home. I rang your doorbell four times short, our code for come down now with your coat already zipped, and raced with you back to the bookstore. I don't remember what I said to you to make you rush. Some nonsense. What I remember is running beside you. The wind that rolled around your body. That it made you all excited, to think you were getting a prophecy. The uplift on your face!

When we got back to the bookstore, the angel on the window ledge was gone. Without him sitting on it, the little shelf looked too narrow to support a whole human.

"Shit," I said, really believing I was losing it, really unsure whether I'd even taught "Angel Levine" that day at all.

But then I looked at you, at your excitement draining from your reddened face, and I said "shit" again, this time because you had wanted a prophecy, too, and I'd gotten one for myself but not for you. I looked at your eyes, so bright in the wind, and that was the first time I saw how sad you were inside.

You looked at my eyes looking at your eyes. You smiled. "Don't ever forget," you said. "When you feel small or afraid, remember: You just ran eight blocks in the cold to tell me we are both known by the angels."

....

Once—the next day, the day you left—I rang your doorbell three thousand times.

....

The angel on stilts—the one in the park, who looked like an angel but wasn't—eventually agreed to kiss me. We negotiated terms, decided we would never try to meet again, convinced ourselves we were chimeras of those we'd lost. (Her daughter and I had both been born on the hottest night of August, to mothers who had never wanted daughters.)

Then she bent over at the waist. The stringy tips of her hair poked through the clouds like a beard through skin, followed by the crown of her head, then the bridge of her nose.

But that was as far as she got. Because she was just a human-sized person up on stilts, bending over at the waist moved her maybe three feet closer to me beside the seesaw. That left a gulf of many stories between us.

I climbed up every rung of the jungle gym. I leapt off, and scaled the nearest tree. I kept on looking at her upside-down eyebrows, growing bigger and bigger each time I took a step up to the next branch.

But at the top of the tree, even puckering my mouth as far out from my face as it would go, I was too far away to kiss her.

She reached down to her ankles. She's been wearing this getup for a while, she said, maybe five years, maybe fifty, but she could still get out of it. She rolled up her jeans and rummaged around at her knees, which were as high as a ten-story building. She couldn't unlatch the strap that anchored the stilts to her calves. I couldn't help her. I watched her fumble. I thought about telling her we could undo our illusions, we weren't you or her daughter at all, but the truth was I'd known that all along and she probably had, too.

She put a hand to her lower back. She straightened up, replacing her head in the clouds. I asked her could she see her daughter in there, but I'm not sure I even believe in the type of heaven where you could just look around and find the friend who is the reason you personally hope heaven exists.

She said she couldn't see anything. Before I climbed back down the tree, I lifted my arms and stood on my tiptoes on the highest branch, so she could kiss a piece of me, but even then I was too low and when I left her she was crying.

I am better in the short form, I have been told since you went away. My stories about loss that start with loss and end with loss are more tolerable when they finish fast.

....

Once, the day I met the angel and you didn't, the temperature dropped in Baltimore. You rang my doorbell two times slow—our code for don't bother with shoes I'm coming up just buzz me in—and walked through my door saying, "What are you doing tomorrow? Let's fly someplace warm." We chose Miami. We researched plane fares, hotels, forecasts, jet-ski rentals. I had a map of the world on my wall, and we plotted, fingertip by fingertip, our path across the planet. We figured out that one of your fingertips scaled to 671 miles on that map. I remember this. Whole cities, the width of your knuckle. My hand was smaller, and covered less distance. This upset you. You pulled up a picture of the earth from space on your phone, and placed my index finger on top of the whole world.

That was the night of the day you hadn't gotten your prophecy. You were quiet, looking at me covering the planet. You were quiet when you said you needed to pick up your suit in case we ate someplace fancy in Miami. I went to the tailor with you, and pointed out while she was in the back room with her tape measure that she had no thumbs. You moaned. In all the years you'd been going to her, you'd never noticed.

I dropped you off at home that night. I said, "Meet you in the morning for the airport." That was the last time I saw you.

....

After I left the park with the angel for my apartment with no neighbors, a year passed. I slept a lot, but I woke up a lot too. I kept on spending half a lifetime looking for you. I kept on finding you piecemeal, in people who sometimes I kissed and sometimes I watched and sometimes I gave money to and sometimes I just played little games inside my head with, like if she drives past my bus by the time it enters the tunnel then you've been looking for me, too.

And then the angel on stilts found me again. It was the first day of spring. She came running like God's chopsticks and stopped at my front porch, where she was taller than the nearest skyscraper. Her papier-mâché wings had mud caked at their tips.

"It's you!" she said.

I laughed. I was so glad to see her. I'd been worried, a little, that she would never stop crying.

"I've got a message," she said, her head in the clouds.

"From the man who's the reason you personally hope heaven exists."

You're dead.

My neighbor, my friend, my person, there was a reason I could never find you in twelve years of looking. Your poet's prophecy must have said you would die before you would ever wake up. I was glad you'd never read it. Standing there at my front door, learning that you'd gone heavenward for real, I felt relief before I felt sorrow—but that doesn't mean relief is what I felt with greater truth. I felt joy, in this life, before I ever felt sadness.

"You saw him up there," I said.

I'd never wanted you to be dead. I'd wanted you to be safe. I'd wanted you to find your prophecy, even if waking up didn't mean you would love me. I'd wanted you, as long as I didn't know about it, to be happy.

"No," she said. "We bumped into each other on the street."

The porch railing felt too tight in my hand.

"Don't cry," said the angel on stilts.

"What did he tell you?" I said. "Where is he? Did he look like I described him? Is he healthy? Is he sad?"

She didn't know.

"Well, is he coming?"

She'd forgotten to have him tag along. He'd been the one to spot her, was the thing, and not vice versa. A couple miles from here, or a couple hundred. Her stilt strides were so long, and she was so high up, she couldn't really tell the difference. She was out of breath. She'd taken off running, because when he saw her he said there was a woman she just had to meet, who lived at this address, who would look at an angel on stilts and remember a happy hopeful running feeling he worries she needs to remember, about an angel she once met outside a bookstore.

"He still remembers this address," I said to the angel on stilts. "He knows I still live here."

The sadness I felt then had its own gravity. Twelve years ago, you walked my hands across the earth. You double-chimed my doorbell and came in. You were my friend. You set up my vacation to Miami, there and back above the clouds, and then you disappeared.

The angel on stilts said, "Yes, he knows." The angel on stilts said, "Oh." She said, "I didn't mean to hurt you." She said, "I think he hoped I'd make you happy."

And then she reared back one long fiberglass leg and kicked it, hard, against the side of my apartment building.

"What are you doing?" I yelled, jumping back into my doorway.

She didn't answer. She kicked again, with her other leg. My attic window shattered.

"Stop!" I said.

But she kept on kicking. Her stilts grew wobbly in the places they connected with the house, and at last, with two great *cracks*, they snapped in two and gravity grabbed her and she fell through the sky to the ground.

And there she was, an angel without stilts in a crumpled

heap in my front yard. Gingerly, I stepped toward her. What would I do if she were dead, and I had to carry you and also an angel on stilts like two stones in my heart?

I reached out toward the heap. I touched the base of the plaster wings on her shoulder, and she stirred. Thank God. She raised her head. For the first time I saw her face, older than I'd imagined, red from the fall and green from the grass. I got overwhelmed with sorrow. She didn't look like you. She didn't look like that other angel on the window ledge. Her papier-mâché wings were dented in three places.

I knelt down in the wood-splintery rubble. I kissed her on the forehead.

"Come inside," I said. "You can play dress-up for me."

"You want me to dress up like him?"

Poor angel on stilts.

"No," I said. "Like you."

Sometimes it feels like there is nothing true to say, except I miss you.

But sometimes there are other things to say. I loved you. There's beauty in that, isn't there? You loved me too, in your way, but you were sad deep inside instead of happy, so all you knew how to do was try and make me think the universe was conspiring in my direction. Sometimes I believe you did it. I believe in every miracle. I believe I know two angels. One wrote a poem about me, and one sleeps on the air mattress in my guest room. We have a system for how we knock on the front door, and she makes me plaster wings, and I tell her all about it, the exhilaration, the running, the knowledge that you and I were poetry. I believe I'm still a little beautiful, if only I would notice. I believe you'll find that old poem and wake up and want to find me. I believe you'll meet your angel. I believe that I've seen Mars.

THE DOCENT

....

In hell there are pockets of places that are worse: more hell.

These are the places where the ashes fall so heavy you can't see. The places where you're close enough to hear the fingernails scraping at the shower ledge. The places where the lice crawl so thick you would go to the barber yourself, bald yourself, to get them off. The places where you think, How dare you vermin feed on what can't feed itself?

Nowhere is there less hell. Only more. This is one of the vicious paradoxes of the camp: more ugliness is possible, but never less.

"Against what, then, do you locate more?" says the Guard, my friend who wants to kill me.

"Against more," I say.

He laughs at me. We are in his house, which sits at the camp's edge, just distant enough from more hell that I can't smell the burning hair. Two pieces of bread sit on a china plate on his mantle. "My little pet," he calls me. It is nice that he calls me this because pets can eat, pets can receive medicine, pets can receive favor, but pets generally cannot fuck. Those prisoners he calls his little loves, to them he is even more friendly.

My Guard goes to the mantle. I feel my heart rise, I am a hungry roadside animal and he will throw me a bite.

"What do you think of this?" he says.

He has picked up a palm-sized painting in a frame beside the plate. I hate the painting. An ugly house of a painting, matte and gray in a steel frame, a painting that is the color of more hell.

"It's beautiful," I say. "Look at the character of the line." He smiles. He gives me one half of one piece of bread. "Beautiful and powerful," I add.

I chew, slowly; the bread is tasteless but for a spot of gray-green mold. He trusts my opinion because in a life before this I was a curator, I was a connoisseur of art, I was a star student of heroic realism. I led young collectors from gallery to gallery in the showrooms of Berlin that popped up even in the sorrows between wars, I watched them go *ooh* and I said things to make them go *ooh* if they didn't go *ooh* loud enough without my persuasion.

"And this one?" he says, holding up a second painting that would be a decent rococo were it not a knockoff. My friend here has been conned by somebody to whom I would offer even a bit of this bread in gratitude and friendship.

"Ooh," I say.

I look out the window. Smoke, barbed wire, a heap of leather shoes taken off the prisoners upon arrival. How do

I extend his questions into the evening without offending him. I want to save something I can do for him for later. I want the second piece of bread, but I don't want it quite yet; I will need to make it last, because my youngest bunkmate died last night and this morning they replaced her with a sharp-eyed baker who sniffed out my hiding place in the wall within minutes. My bunk, now, has become more hell.

"That good?" he says, of the forgery. He is looking at me with the type of deference I don't want him ever to become aware of, because the moment he becomes aware of it he will kill me. I know where his deference comes from. I have a secret which has made me almost a celebrity with my Guard. Though I have neither confirmed nor denied, he has good reason to suspect that I took art classes years ago with a certain very special German celebrity. I have direct knowledge of the man who is my Guard's God.

I must be very careful with this knowledge. When your protector's God failed to gain entrance to classes that you passed with ease, you dispense your information in strategic little chunks.

"Tell me," he says, considering the fake. "What was the Führer's favorite color?"

"Palette," I say, to stall. "What was his favorite palette."

The Guard too is looking out the window. He is nervous. There have been rumors lately that liberation is coming, rumors that the guards are trying to march shoeless groups of us away to our deaths before liberation can come. But there have also been rumors that they want to march us to our deaths for fun, another form of more hell, blisters that turn water to blood as surely as Jesus turned water to wine. There have been rumors that the rumors of liberation are just some new prisoner's yellow-aching hope. The one thing here that is impossible for them to murder.

Me, I've killed my hope for a better existence. That is why I can sit with the Guard and chat about not-art here, in the ugliest place in the world. This is what life is now, and I will cling to this nothing with all my heart. I will not give them the satisfaction of throwing myself too soon into the ovens. What I lack in hope I make up for in spite. I will not do them the favor of making it any easier to snuff me out.

"His favorite palette was blue and gold," I say, which is the truth. He liked seascapes and beach houses, I remember this. But he was a terrible artist, completely visionless. He painted buildings the way a contractor draws blueprints for a municipal hall, not the way an architect dreams of impossible palaces in the sky. This is one gift I can give myself: Hitler was an awful artist. I know, I remember how he used to ache with wanting to be good at painting. He wanted to succeed at art with the force with which I want to cling to this gnarled-up animal life. I hope it pains him, in whatever four-poster bed he shares with Satan, that no matter how many he kills in his rage that he was not good, he will never be good. No matter how many sycophants tell him he is smart or powerful, he will never make anything that is beautiful. Look at this place. Even the scalps poking through our hair are indistinct and gray.

"Blue and gold," the Guard repeats. Maybe he is thinking what I am thinking: And how did that turn black and red?

Outside, a sudden commotion. I see it as a shimmer of heat in the air, I hear it as a flurry of gunshots, I understand it as: more hell. A guard I don't know comes running to the door.

"Leave," says my Guard, hastily replacing his painting above the mantle. But I have no chance to leave. The door in front of me is the door to which the guard is running. I bend over the arm of a chair to spare my Guard the embarrassment of having asked me about art, so that is how the new guard sees me and understands me in relation to my Guard, one of the many collections of bones that he calls his little loves.

"An English speaker," says the stranger. "Now."

"Has it happened?" says my Guard.

They look at each other for a long time. The eagle atop their helmets, splayed in plated gold, looks dead. My Guard swallows.

"You," says my Guard to me. "What did they teach you in that art school of yours?"

I straighten up. I have to decide whether to blend in or stand out. These are the choices that determine life or death, here in hell; sometimes each choice corresponds to one and sometimes the other.

I say, in German, "They taught me English."

"Good," says the stranger. "Come with me."

·········

I am told that there is a person to whom I must show the camp. I am told that this person does not want the guards to show him around; he wants a prisoner to do it. What kind of perversion, I think, what kind of more hell, in what dark corners does he want to spit on me. Standing out was death today, I chose wrong, today I will be the fingernails shrieking down the shower ledge.

But the guard leads me to the entrance of my bunk, and there my eyes are overcome with green: soldiers with the flag of the United States sewn on their arms. A man in a suit and tie stands in the middle of them. How long it has been since I have seen a suit and tie and not a uniform; I had forgotten how rectangular the shoulders, how triangular the point of the tie, such geometric brutalism. The man has a long oval head and insistent ears and eyes used to being sad.

"You are the English speaker," says the man, in American-accented English. His voice is kind.

I nod. Was standing out life today, after all? Another paradox of hell: the same choice that was death this morning is life this afternoon and can be death again this evening. Every choiceless choice is life and death, both.

"My name is Edward Murrow," he says, and he extends his hand.

I recoil. For long seconds I stand with my palm spread like a shield above my face, ready for the blow, before I remember that in another lifetime men who stood with brooding eyes and perfect poise in the entrance to my gallery used to shake my hand.

Too late, I reach toward him.

His sad eyes do not get sadder; they get alert. His hand leaves the air between us and goes to the pen and notebook in his breast pocket. I understand now: I have given him an image. My bad-dog's fear will be an image for some story he will write about his visit to this strange museum of death. He is here to make a transaction: he will give me the temporary safety of standing with the Americans, I will give him material. I know transaction, here in hell. Art for bread. Yet this Edward Murrow reminds me less of my Guard and more of my old buyers in the gallery: men who would talk with me, offer their hand, ask where I was from, but all the time their eyes were darting to the prints and the frames and the ways I might move to give the true value away.

Murrow says, "I am a radio reporter and I'd like to tell the world about this place." He slides the pen behind his ear and the notebook into his pocket. "Would you show me around?"

"Of course," I say. "Welcome," I say. Am I free, I almost say, but the words catch in my throat.

"Wherever you want to begin," he says.

I take him to the entrance of my barrack. Inside: five to a bunk, cracking wooden bedframes, tattered blankets where there are blankets at all, the baker woman new this morning lying very still at a strange angle to the wall.

I hear a muffled gagging sound beside me. I look at Murrow. His eyes are retracting inward, pupils dilating, all horror. But he looks back at me and adopts an even kinder voice when he says, "Tell me."

What does he want me to say? This is not yet even more hell.

"There," I say, pointing to the middle bunk. There a man who'd snuck into the women's side once tried to hold me, and I bit him in the armpit where it looked like his body might have stored a little meat. "There we sleep," I say, "and wake up every morning for roll call."

Murrow does not take out his pen. If I am not helpful to him, if I fail to give him the images he wants, then maybe he will leave and the guards will be angry that I volunteered to see him and standing out will have been death after all.

"There," I say again. I move my finger up an inch, so I am pointing to the wall that abuts the middle bunk. "There is the crevice where I hide some extra bread, when I can find it."

This seems to stir him.

"You must be hungry," he says, and he withdraws a small sucking candy from that glorious breast pocket. The crinkling of the wrapper is the loudest thing I've heard in years. The crystal is sweet on my tongue.

Murrow watches me as though he might cry. This man who has given me candy for so little work. Please don't be sad, I want to say. I am a tour guide of hell, my dear friend, you are with me, I know every crevice of this place. Here is where they beat us. Here is where they burn us. Here is where they count us.

"Here is where I found a place to write," I say, pointing now to the underside of the bunk above mine, not saying I stole a stub of pencil from the desk of my Guard when he wasn't looking. "I drew a game of hangman."

Murrow narrows his eyes at the plank of wood where I used up every half centimeter of lead. I do not want him to be horrified. I want him to notice the perfect circle of the head I have drawn, I want him to notice the perfect proportions of the squeezed-shut eyes, the heroic realism of the hanging man I drew because my youngest bunkmate couldn't guess my word because I never picked one. "I followed the grain of the wood to draw a straight line to the gallows," I say.

Murrow doesn't look at me; he makes a note in his little pad. I have impressed him. A stab of something wonderful and dormant in my chest. The feeling I used to have when I knew a buyer would leave and tell his friends, send Christmas cards, stock the back room with the heaviest beer. I vow to impress him again.

"Come," I say. I lead Murrow outside, where the American soldiers close in tight as lice around us. From behind my Guard's house I hear explosions, I hear shouting too robust to be the meek final protests of the starving. "I will show you something that will really," I say, and I pause, trying to remember a phrase I read once in an English primer, "knock your shoes off."

"How did you live here," Murrow murmurs, and again I want to tell him: This is a place of paradox. The only way to live is to give up on life. If you love life too much, if you find it too beautiful, then you cannot survive such ugliness; if out there you invested too much in beauty that is denied you, then to live here you must embrace ugliness.

And with this, something monstrous comes over me, another stab from that dormant place in my chest, I feel tears rise from a place long dry. This time I can recognize the feeling: hope. Maybe after all I will emerge from this place, human again, how strangely easy to slip back into my human form, to find a place within me that is less hell.

I want to show Murrow the barrack from the front, because I think I can impress him with the ease of the architecture, the clean line. Along the way I see a very skinny woman lying on her back, gazing unblinking at the airplanes that are clouding in the sky. I didn't know her. I notice the deep, saturated red of her blood.

Beside me, Murrow moans.

"What am I looking at?" he asks me.

"The form," I say, astonished still by the hope that keeps stabbing with more frequency and force. I close my eyes, not even looking, remembering truly for the first time what it was like to lead a lover of art through a profusion of beauty. "Below the neck," I say, "where you expect a breast to push out, we have here intaglio." It has been lifetimes since I have spoken the elegant Italian words of art in a tone of sincerity. "A sculpture sunken in," I explain.

I open my eyes. Murrow is staring at me very strangely, his mouth partly open, his pen unmoving above his notebook. I have come alive again, my friend, I want to tell him, out of hell I have reclaimed my life, I am a docent again my friend, I have escaped this hell of paradox.

"Intaglio," says Murrow, as though in a trance, as though the soft roll of the language is impossible to fathom.

"Instead of," I begin. With my hands I try to show protrusion, a sculpture taking up space. I struggle for the word in English. "Relief."

At this he exchanges a raised eyebrow with one of the soldiers. Will he give me another sucking candy, I wonder, have I yet given him the perfect image?

"Hitler is a devil," he says. But it is me he's looking at as he begins to weep.

"Hitler," I say—and I wonder how my Guard will fare with the Americans, and I look up to a sky of blue and a sun glinting gold off the spread wings of the airplanes—"is a very great artist."

I AM GOING TO LOSE
EVERYTHING I HAVE
EVER LOVED

....

We begin with facts: You loved me first. Before you knew it, you have come to say. From the instant you saw me. This story of yours, of course, is a fairytale. You only smiled at a girl-who-could-have-been-any-girl on a bridge, river flowing under her, traffic rushing behind her, brown curly hair and an hourglass her dress wasn't trying to hide.

Of course, I believe you loved me from the instant you saw me and centuries before. Time bends, Samuel, in a story that is true. All our love was packed into that first smile.

No. No, you are going to leave me, and when you do you aren't coming back. I am susceptible to letting myself get carried away. Hope can carry me a long way—to another story, where my fury makes you choose me. This is my problem, my Friend says over coffee now, that I'm incapable of anger in the presence of its object. She sets her mug on the windowsill with a light clink. The barista loves her; I'm drinking from a paper cup that says "dinah" without a capital, and he's already bringing her a fresh pot of cream. Nonetheless she's right. I can sit in a coffee shop reporting my anger, but before you I can only laugh or beg or hope. Hope: that murderer. The unmet longing that my heart bangs its head against. Hope is the bubbles in Willy Wonka's chocolate factory, and truth is the fan waiting to chop my head off. Kill it. Hope for nothing and live. My Friend should not fetishize hope. It wasn't hope that kept her going in the camps, my Nana Itta always said. "Why then did you live," I would ask her—trying not to sob, because even as a teenager, all I felt when I was with her was the hope that the next time I saw her I would bring a man who would raise children with me, so she would know I was going to keep our family alive even after they had killed us.

Why then did she live? "It's life," she would say. The *because* somewhere built in. I know she felt we were surrounded by ghosts, she and I as we sat in her living room. My unmade cousins right there with us, tapping on the glass. I felt them sometimes, too. The night Samuel and I first slept together in the B&B behind the bridge—I never told him this—I felt the ghosts lying in bed beside us. Then flattening themselves to hover in the ever smaller space between us. Then pressing their pinky fingertips inside me along with his, which was a good feeling, it was what made me so willing to bring him inside without asking questions.

They were staking their claim, coming too. When he came I thought of Nana, I thought thank God, I suppose that was when I loved him.

As soon as I rolled off of him I told him I'd never done that before, and I was never going back to doing it the old way. "Do what, Dinah?" he said, and I said, "Fuck without a condom." He was flabbergasted. But I'd been so confident about it, I'd climbed right on, I hadn't paused. "And I'm not on birth control either," I added—and where he should have blanched, he laughed, which may also have been when I loved him. I sensed it already: the more outrageous the better, with this one. Good, because I was in constant outrage. Love hadn't come to me. I was thirty-seven. I had tried. What I felt was worse than outrage, it was the truth of loneliness, but it is too early in this story to understand the texture of that.

He laughed, and stroked my pinky fingertip slowly with his own, and I told him I had a good explanation for my oversight about the condom: I was ovulating. I only realized it as I was telling him. With him my body tried to meet its needs without my notice, and when I noticed, maybe that was when I loved him.

I would have written *that was why I loved him*, but that line is never true. I loved him because by the time I could meet him I had already loved him from the beginning of time. That he is a sad singer, a political savant, a logistical basket case, that he draws maps of imaginary kingdoms where his father is the king, that he has a hollow collarbone and a dexterous tongue—the explanations for love are always playing catch-up to the fact of it.

So I was ovulating the first time he and I had sex: my genes' need to replicate and my spirit's need to pair and my Nana's ghosts' maniacal need to break out from behind the glass, wailing in my arms—they worked together to overcome all those decades of education that couldn't do either of the two things I wanted, anyway, which was make me not-alone or keep me safe. Forget barriers, my body said. My Nana's ghosts overtook me, he was here, my brain was elsewhere.

I didn't miss it.

So it was life that kept my Nana going in the camps, that was all, not a gift but a fact, like the laws of physics or of gravity. You are given life, you tend it. You are struck on the knee, your leg jumps. An effect without a cause beyond the physical source. You need not hope for better to tend the life you have. God gave it: hate him for it, love him for it, disbelieve in him or spit on him or try to find his mother; you have it now.

So when Samuel said later that, unless I let him leave his wife for me slowly over time—time I didn't have before my Nana's ghosts came screaming out my throat—he would kill himself, I didn't take him seriously. A gamble. My Friend's first boyfriend had threatened to kill himself if she left him; she did; he did. Blew his skull off. Now she can't say no to anyone. She is the best friend a selfish person could ask for.

(I am not a selfish person, she would have me clarify. She knows I tend to make myself the villain in the story. Lightly villainous, obnoxious more than immoral, which is worse if you are a woman wanting a man. She would have me note that I rented a car and drove her to the mental hospital, when she had to go, and that I removed my shoelaces and belt and drawstrings alongside her, and I checked her in, and stayed inside with her when the fire alarm screamed and the patients had to stay and the visitors could leave. All this is true. I am excellent at showing up for friends when they are miserable. I will raise them up until their happiness repulses me. I will cover their ears against the voices but I will never, ever remember their wedding anniversaries. I make it a point to forget.)

I haven't shared Nana's story with Samuel. He came along too late to meet her, and for this I always hated him. God I will miss him. How many ways are there to deal with longing. I want to lance it. I want to throw it up. It lives in that place at the top of my collarbone, where nausea sits. (Do not think of his collarbone.) It wants to be expelled. (This is my reality story, flights of fancy don't belong here, they make the impossible seem possible. His collarbone was a birth defect, it stuck out too far and made his shoulder thin and sloping on his left side and was hollow. It was a genetic anomaly. It was like he was a bird.)

I don't know why I haven't told him Nana's story. Her story isn't one I keep secret. I write it freely in fictional and nonfictional ways, I am liberal about calling one the other,

I only half-know it and feel no compunction about changing it to suit my story's needs. Mine were the last eyes on her before the coffin closed, so I feel a certain ownership. With strangers the story comes up often. It came up with two Belgian girls I met in a bar once, who cried and said they would never forget it or me or my Nana and whose names I can't remember.

But with you, Samuel, never. Her story explains me, I told the two Belgians. It explains why sorrow is always waiting under my joy but joy is not always under my sorrow, why I haven't been able to find a man to have children with, my suspicion of laws and banks and national anthems and hope. I guess my sorrow and my hopelessness come up a lot, with other people. I find myself having to explain them. You, though. Samuel, you are the origin story of my happiness. With you I open my mouth to tell the story and a song-note comes out instead, and I can't bring you a death story. So I say that today my father and I freed a mouse we caught under a cup in my kitchen. I let you tell me my heart is loving toward the small things of this world. I do not say that we'd both prefer to snap the vermin's neck, but we drive the highway with its feet on our lap because we are Nana's. To shorten a life is a sin.

Of course it's my own fault, this mess with you. I should not have gotten mixed up with a man who was already mixed up with a woman. Heading straight for immoral, more than obnoxious. I won't try such a thing again. But you smiled at me on that bridge, and all the hoped-for men before you disappeared. Oh, I thought. This is what it looks like when a person loves me. I understand now, why I could never logic anyone else into this smile.

I did, at the time. I did think that. Time had folded. We hadn't met yet. He already loved me; I already knew.

He came so easily to loving me that it seemed impossible his relationship was not in some way already over. Surely, at least, it had to be on its way out. I knew better than these hopeful surelys, of course. I'd had the gift of watching my Friend and my cousin and my schoolmates dating endless men; maybe five years younger than Samuel, maybe two inches taller, most were similarly inclined to run from life instead of grabbing it by the throat. I should have known to be wary, when a man lives in a life he needs to run from. So this mess I'm in now is my own fault. Samuel has never blamed me, for what it's worth. He never says I knew what I signed up for. God I love him. It will be impossible to end. I know the hard truth that my Friend will not acknowledge: to lose him does not mean I will find someone else. It could be all loss, all the way down. This is possible. Has been possible. Out of this hard truth I once wrote an essay that was picked up by the *Baltimore Sun* that was picked up by a group of angry online men—incels, they call themselves, involuntary celibates—who hate me, which is funny, because they and I have more in common in our righteous loneliness than not. I empathize with them. They do not empathize with me, because I have written an article that calls for men to allow women to leave them without so much as a peep. I wrote the article in honor of my Friend. After it I am no longer allowed to make peeps when men try to leave me, or else I am a hypocrite of the highest order, and so I come to learn that sitting back and accepting the unknowable reasons behind the will of others is more difficult than I could have possibly imagined.

For me, Samuel. Never for you.

Your brother is the loneliest man in the world. This sounds like invention for story, but it is not. This is my only-truth story, my only one. He reads books about World War II and he lives beside your parents in a house they bought for him and he quits every job you manage to wrangle him into with his associate's degree in hospitality. When I am asked out by one of those online men, who sends me unanswered message after unanswered message and uses Twitter to announce his bafflement that the entitled fucking bitches of DC/Baltimore do not like him, I am reading his texts out loud to you, to show you how scary he is, and you tell me to stop. You can't stand it. His words are someone else's private calling-out, they are not for you to know. You tell me your brother once posted a rage to Facebook, asking why nobody bothered to click a button and wish him happy birthday. You tell me to be gentle with this person's heart.

So it is to other people that I say I am afraid this man will show up at my apartment someday and blow my head off. To you I let him disappear from the stories we tell each other, even as we praise ourselves for our ability to tell each other everything, and I regard you with yet another layer of confounding goodness. This seeing of your brother everywhere, in every loneliness except mine, is of a piece with the impenetrable puzzle shapes of your map-making and your castle-dreaming and your bird collarbone. They are the gentlenesses of you. They have nothing to do with your anti-anxiety prescription rising higher the longer you carry on with me. No, these are the parts that make me long to watch you from the doorway in a house we share, you hunched over a drawing table with your tongue between your lips, me going over to kiss the top of your head. It is to less gentle people that I speak of how dangerous it is to be a single woman, not because we will be followed home by a stranger who knows he is a stranger, but because we will be followed home by a stranger who thinks he is a suitor.

Once many years ago, a man who was a stranger became the man who would become my Nana's husband because he showed up at her doorstep, unannounced. She was in hiding behind a false wall in a pantry. He'd found out she was there because she had the look of someone who was not the woman on her papers, and he'd trailed her home. (All half-knowing. How are both truths true, that she was hiding and also walking home?) One part is certain: when she came to the door, he held out a piece of cellophane wrapping in his hand. It was a time of stale bread and dried milk, and in the middle of the war he brought her nougat.

It is doing of this kind that will ruin me-and-Samuel finally. Talking to him is well and good, feeling the immensity of this thing between us is well and good, as is making bold claims to our uniqueness. That our love springs from a well of absolute equality, which is insanity. True equal partnership is necessarily insanity. It means we don't know how to do each other. Somebody should be certain, somebody should be the less fumbling one.

In some ways it has been me. My strength in love is creativity, in a complex relationship I am finally able to shine. Distance, affair, age gap, anxiety—I have become expert at figuring out a third way. I love it. Maybe I need it. I am able to find pockets of possibility that other people don't even look for. Five a.m. Sublets near his home in Boston. Hotels in the next town over. Kennels for his dog. I can bend the rules of the civilized world because I don't really believe in civility, and so have kept myself on its periphery. It is always easier to see the fissures from the outside.

Was it Nana who taught me this, that the rules of civility break down so I may as well ignore them, get a head start at seeing the cabinets and attics and false papers of the world?

But my two cousins are my Nana's other grandchildren: the older one drops one man for the next like clothes into the laundry; the younger one is married, to a standard man with a standard vision of loosely equal love. So it must be me who took what Nana had to tell—guns, gas, train tracks—and decided, oh, the rules are broken. If they will break me later, I will disavow them now.

So he and I have met at five a.m., and in hotels and sublets and pockets of time I point out and he accepts with such gusto that it makes equality from the fact that the suggestions had been mine. We have loved this way, and surely ours is equal to more standard forms of love, if different—and this is believable, until other people's alive new boyfriends run into a coffee shop carrying the depression meds they've left unswallowed on the bedside table. Or show up at their doorstep in the middle of a war. Or sit beside them at their little cousin's wedding, which was in June, and very sad. When other people do that, then I feel something shift inside me and the truth reveals itself: the immense way he and I have loved is not enough. It isn't even love. It isn't nougat.

Sometimes I'm furious at chance or God for this. If anyone had loved me when I was younger, then maybe now, two decades into adulthood, I wouldn't be coming from a place of constant scarcity and so would not accept other people's husbands and so love would not be constantly scarce. Cruel, that love comes most readily to those who have had it before. Samuel said so, once. One thing among the thousands that worried him about exchanging her for me was that I'd never lived with a boyfriend. Do I understand about sharing a bathroom? About the way a hair that clogs the shower drain can interrupt even the most passionate of intertwinings? That worry broke me like a rule. "Don't punish me for that," I told him. "Don't give me more nothing because I've had nothing."

A metaphor about job security, maybe. How you need experience to get experience. Who cares. Jobs mean nothing.

That's another truth my Friend does not like or want to believe—she met alive new boyfriend at a sales meeting, have I considered getting a real job, in an office—and it's another reason I want so much that my wanting becomes too ugly to allow me to get. Jobs mean nothing. Only love means anything. I say this knowing that people starve. With money or without it, with civility or without it. Nana knew too. In the middle of the war her husband brought her nougat, and when he died, losing him stood just as impossibly in her heart as losing her entire village, her entire family, her God himself for the rest of her life. And so I hold my life soft and fluid and open, like legs, until there is anyone worth concretizing for.

You. How I have learned you, Samuel. Your cartographies of imaginary worlds, your portraits of your father in the basement, your laugh. A guffaw that defined the word, I had only read about guffaws. You drew me cartoon queendoms. You sang your messages on my voicemail. I listened to them like the radio. I made up a song that made you giggle. When we shared hotel rooms we had an easy ritual around poop: I sang the song that I made up for you, I turned up the TV, you laughed when you emerged.

See. I could have understood it, about bathrooms.

I am afraid beyond fear that you will never show up in a coffee shop for me. I am afraid I know the texture of the reason. The only thing I want to do is sing to you. Take your head on my chest and pet your hair until you are sleeping. "It's a maternal love," says my Friend, having swallowed her meds and watched her boyfriend leave the coffee shop. She says this ignoring all the stories I have told her about Nana, ignoring that I know no Jewish mother who accepts her children for exactly who they are. "Give that love to yourself," says my Friend, who is no longer alone and refuses to remember what it was like. No one loves themselves the way they do their child or their lover. No one wants to kiss themselves on the forehead.

"You think being in a relationship is so great?" says the barista, who has overheard and is in love with her and may have just found out that she has an alive new boyfriend. He is wiping his hands too forcefully on his apron. He is probably with a partner he doesn't love. Or else one who doesn't love him, with whom the sex has stopped or never existed or should never have existed, with whom he has nothing to talk about. Maybe one who annoys him, which is the true opposite of love. Impossible to feel amorous when someone is an irritation on a couch. Over the years, I have told a friend or two that they only stay with their passionless partners out of fear of being me, alone. I tell them sometimes it is worse to fear the bogeyman than to be him.

After that, those friends and I lose touch.

Your brother. I called it early: I heard the way you talked about him, and I heard that there is something familial in your love for me, too. I am your brother, I heard this early, earlier than you though you will come to it eventually. "My parents try to make him feel so loved," you said. "They let him read to them about World War II, not novels or histories, just facts, aviation parts and train numbers and rifle suppliers. He doesn't narrate with inflection either, it's hard for him to read emotion in person, even harder on a page. He just drones, and my mom says uh-huh and stirs the chicken into broth, and my dad says what else and claps the mud off his shoes. My dad is eighty-seven. Iz is forty-three."

It is a kind of grace, what your parents do for him. We both agree. It is graceful and also sad. They do for him what I do for you: tell you I love everything about you, the things I don't love too, because such totality makes you so happy that I am willing to love the things I don't love if it draws that happiness out of you. These are the delicate conditionals of love, I am learning, so often the contingent on contingent: If you want it, I want it; if it makes you happy, it makes me happy; if you love to be loved, I will love you.

But your parents will fail. There is no substitute for this, the kind of love I give to you. I know it. My father is my Nana's son, he loves me so and all I can do in his presence is long for you to meet him. Your father does for your brother what my father does for me, which is not enough: invites me home for New Year's, says he is thrilled to see me, reminds me I was born with my eyes open in his arms. But I am unpleasant to him in every way when I am tossing in the twin bed of my childhood, knowing my one cousin is off with his Christian in-laws and my other cousin is lying in the beds of a growing list of men and my Nana who is dead now would be crying, *But who will have the grandchildren?*

and she would mean, *But who will bring our ghosts into existence out between our legs.*

I have tried to think of how to help your brother. Of who I know who might accept a set-up. Someone intimate with loneliness. Someone who doesn't take another human heart beside theirs for granted. A woman whose brother is sad. That man, the one who scared me. Me. I have thought about this, truly, whether it could be me. But to love him would be an act of loving you, and the only kind that could be enough denies the rules of transitive property or substitution.

Who doesn't take another human heart beside theirs for granted. That's your problem, Samuel. Your hardest story is the one where two people love you. You and I are different species. You'd have had to make me human.

I have thought of writing him a letter:

Isidore of the beautiful name,

I am a friend of your brother's. You haven't heard of me. Once, your brother sobbed in my lap and said it's you who deserves the kind of love I give to him. He doesn't; you do. He loves you so. Not enough to live like you do, of course. Soon he'll be leaving me. I know how lonely you must be. He doesn't; I do. I swear I do. There is nothing more to say. He doesn't love you, it's true. You and I both know it.

P.S. It would devastate him if he knew.

"He doesn't respect the shortness of all this," says my Friend. The barista has unnerved her with the force of his removing the cream from our table, and she has decided suddenly that she is willing to get it. She waves her arms to encompass herself and me, the barista and the coffee shop, greater Baltimore, the United States of America, the earth and sky and all of time immemorial. "He doesn't respect that death is coming, and love is the only thing." There is no greater goodness. It is a sin to leave me, if you love me. There is no order of morality beyond this.

The wife, perhaps, would disagree.

I have been to her home. Met and pet and even walked her dog, who should have bitten me but didn't. I did not sit on her furniture. I stood in the middle of rooms, I kept my hands in my pockets, I did not look at the books in the bookshelves or the pictures in the frames. I understand you, sister. Usually I write fiction. There I can bear to look and see that you and he are smiling and natural and guffawing together at somebody's cousin's wedding. There, maybe, you can bear to look and see that the number he says is his father, calling all the time, is not the number from which his father calls you. Sometimes we do not want to know the things we already know.

Or maybe we don't know. Samuel, you tell me Anne loves you, in her way. The truth is I believe she loves you and I believe you love her and I believe you love me and I am almost certain I love you with the brutality and totality that I promise you, up and down and sideways, whispering in your ear, gasping it, mumbling. Sex. The partner's name too beautiful. An angel's name, too foreign to speak, a name I use when I am angry or playful or telling him to tell me to get down on my knees. We are excited by each other's excitement, our sexuality is a law of infinite recursion. We invent positions that we both know have probably been invented before. We name them after the places we invented them, Hen of the Wood, Malaprop, Blue Orchid, and so they are ours, filled like our bodies with history and desire.

"But Dinah," says my Friend. She signals for a second coffee. The barista, sighing, pulls out another mug. "Obeying desire isn't the way you attain desire. Restraint is the way."

But here's the thing—Isidore already knows—when you are the child of who we are children of, other people's counsel is as useless as their rules. Other people stayed in the Gestapo's office and were carted to the camps; my Nana's husband saw the officer turn his back and swiped a piece of candy off his desk and walked right out. Other people tell me to say no to Samuel, make him wait, make him work—but where is the joy in restraint?

"The joy is in the power," says my Friend. "You get to keep the power."

As if there is only one kind of power. There is power in offering, owning yourself so completely that you can give yourself away. Recklessness is a form of power. The unexpected yes. The all the way. The take my heart take my body have my future take my life, take it, I trust you for no reason, I ask you to prove nothing, I sense only that what is divine in me resonates at the pitch of what is divine in you, and that your definition of sin will be letting me go.

My conundrum way back on the bridge, knowing already that he had the satiated look of a man whom another woman loves: take something, or keep nothing. When you have had only nothing, you know there's nothing worse. You will take anything. You will never say no. You will walk back every line in the sand: Sit next to me in June; Decide by October; See me on New Year's, do it, I'm through.

When you've had only nothing, you'll never be through. Ask Isidore of the beautiful name. To go back to nothing is the worst thing. It is no one to hold you. The knowledge that babies die if no one touches them. Three a.m., four a.m., no difference. One p.m. even worse. You know that three a.m. is coming.

Not you, of course, Samuel. You are a different species. I've tried and sputtered every time, to offer you this intimacy: that ghosts live over my shoulder behind a glass wall that separates the living from the dead. You've watched me with those well-loved eyes and I've known your lot is too much with the living. Some things are too sad for you, and this is even sadder, in the way that all things that are sad become sadder: there's no hope of change. The ghosts were all set to be created, in the middle of the last century, but they never got to be. The wombs and arms and hands that were supposed to shepherd them into the world got gassed or shot or tossed into a pit. The ghosts didn't know where to go. God wouldn't take them back or else they wouldn't have him, I don't know, the theology is crooked and Nana never trafficked in theology. Me neither, not here. And so they stand behind my family and press their noses to the glass like gorillas in a zoo. Then they press their way in between bodies that are forming positions that only feel new, they sneak into the egg and sperm and they live and grow and emerge out between our legs.

They try to, anyway. But these are sad ghosts, they have spent eons separated from the world, we both know people who can understand them. These unmade of my uncles and aunts and cousins, they try so hard, where there is too much life, to pass through the glass: when my Nana and her husband who brought nougat are conceiving their sons; when her son and my mother who doesn't pet my hair are conceiving their daughter. For the most part, the ghosts fail. They were meant for an earlier century and they do not thrive in the unnatural heat of this one. Barely anybody even sees them. My mother and cousins don't, my father only sometimes. Nana used to ask.

Maybe you are suspecting already, my guess as to the truth of loneliness. I am coming to it. My journalism teacher told me once that I was crazy, that I am full of wilderness and abundance and grace, that I carry these things with me when I step into a room. I am life in a dizzying verdure, she said, and if I choose to be anything else it's only a story I tell myself, and I better stop, soon.

If I don't stop then time will loop back. Samuel's first smile will also contain the loss of him. I will be unable to recall that to love him is to feel I have always been waiting to be conceived of through the eyes of a man who dreams of castles. Isidore, this is time as you will never know it. Your brother's love will never teach you as it teaches me, the love you have is not the kind that teaches. Here's another lesson: nouns. Nouns are of utmost importance, when the person you love is not beside you and you wish to tell him how you wish to hold him. In person you simply touch his cheek, or collarbone, or uppermost protruding bone of collarbone, or base of penis. You need not name it. But in the distance between Baltimore and Boston, you learn that there are infinite places to touch your lover's hand, but there are finite nouns. Palm, wrist, fist, finger, knuckle, thumb. Words like "pinky" are useless, add no value from a distance, only a level of ridiculousness, though in person the slow stroking of a pinky finger can be the most erotic or loving or suggestive or sorrowing gesture in the world.

Compound nouns, too, Iz. There are endless available joinings of a noun to its diminutive, babylove, babybird, gorillababy. Your brother and I never use each other's names. Our public names, he calls them. When I speak the word "Samuel" it feels foreign in my mouth. Once I was looking at him and I forgot his name. He told me that was the most intimate thing on earth. Then he told me that in college, at a summer job his dad had gotten him, he'd sold furniture. I picture him younger, blond, insouciant, knowing or sensing he had the world—I do not think I would have liked him, he was too sure that love was coming—selling people the nouns that would tie them to the floors and homes and co-couch-buyers I would fight, someday, to have him.

I do not think I would have liked him, I was too sure that love was not coming.

Back when my Friend was sadder, she read a made-up story of mine that I'd mailed to the institution. In response, she asked if I had ever been in love. She asked this through a tinny phone connection, which annoyed me, because I had just waited for an hour as the wall phone in her ward had been passed from hand to hand. "The inmates running the asylum," I had muttered to my father. He had laughed. I called her maybe twice more while she was in there. Later, when she was out and taking sales meetings, she told me that my father had called her every day.

Something authentic was missing from the romance, was what my Friend had to say about my story. I couldn't tell then what it was. It was pet names. The woman called her lover by his name, which was all wrong but I didn't know. There used to be a scene where the woman yelled at the man, saying "I love you too" are the best words in the English language, because they contain reciprocation baked in. I thought this was wise, when I wrote it. I thought I was wise.

I was wrong. There are some wisdoms that extrapolation

and study and guesswork can teach; others require experience. It turns out there are gradations of the best words in the English language: when felt deeply, I answer "I love you" with "I love you," as if coming to the discovery yet again for the first time. I don't say "too." I could not have guessed this. Of course then I am bitter, that I won't keep this love. A whole font of wisdom I won't access. Instead, I grow wiser about loneliness.

Not as wise as Isidore of the beautiful name, though. Never as wise as your loneliest man in the world.

....

Nana's story: a set piece, it turns out. I never share it with Samuel. I never know it, fully. Judaism teaches that to save one person is to save a world. I use Nana's story to explain myself and so to explain the world. I use it to prop my learnings up on stacks of nougat. The foundation of my lessons is gunpowdery and soft.

My Friend counsels to approach my situation in a lighter tone. "You're funny," she tells me. "Remember?"

I just look at her there stirring her second coffee with a genteel little spoon. A live new boyfriend is on the couch in their apartment, waiting for her to come home. I remember holding her cotton pants around her waist with my hands, because they made her take out the drawstrings. I remember them locking us behind a sliding-glass door while the fire alarm screamed.

"Sure," I say. "But men-and-women aren't funny."

"I know," she says, "I know, it's all tragedy. Just . . . laugh about it."

"Nougat," I tell her. "That's a funny word. Funnier than chocolate, which is what the candy was. I'll use nougat instead of chocolate. Fuck truth."

"That's some mild humor," says my Friend.

Because I can't laugh. Nothing will be tactical, in the end. The time for tactics will have been before, when I had him, when I had the luxury of pretending I was another kind of girl, one not so intimate with loneliness, a girl on the side of life. It is a sin, I'll tell him, in the end. I'll be on my knees, he'll be telling me about dignity or civility, I'll be telling him there is no civil way to break my heart. It's a sin, I'll say. We are for each other. Life is for this.

But you can't teach what is sinful to a man who doesn't know. If you find yourself needing to, you've already lost. The only counsel I'm certain of: find a man who agrees with your definition of sin. Obeying orders. Killing mice. Leaving your friend when the firing squad screams. Leaving love to just die on the table.

Sin: an abomination against what is holy. To find a man who agrees with your definition of sin, you must first find a man who agrees with your definition of holiness. Sex. Poop songs. The slow stroking of a pinky finger. When he leaves, I will once again be a woman denied what is holy in this life. How many times can I be sinned against before it's clear it's me who is the sinner?

Your brother. To keep loving me would be to love him,

Samuel, don't you see that? I would have fed it into him. Don't ask me how. We're coming to it. Maybe you already know, or guess. In the Torah, El is one god, Yahweh another. Some insist they are one and the same; whole schools of ancient rabbis lived and died to cover up their difference, to knit them together like the ring of darker skin at the head of your penis from your circumcision. What hell if they were two, because true equal partnership is necessarily insanity. Co-equal gods cannot exist. They will war for dominance and one will win. I never asked Nana what she thought, if our gods were one or two. I think she would have hoped they were two; she had enough hatred for two gods, it would explain her overflow of rage.

And now I live with clenched fists because her overflow pools in me. Because Isidore—Iz—: I am going to lose everything I have ever loved. It turns out love is both mineral and animal, Iz. Bedrock and breathing. And love is law, too. Laws of sin and blessing; laws of physics; most of all, the law of perpetual motion.

Iz, it turns out what's most frightening about love is how alive it is. You'll think you have a handle on it, this little golden city inside your chest. You learn the shape and structures of love as you learn its object's body: shyly at first, then bolder, laughingly, audaciously, abundantly. And so you come to know love's geographies, the places it has studs and fault lines, where it is load-bearing—then suddenly your Friend leaves you alone in a coffee shop and goes home to her boyfriend, and you feel it shift inside you. You are alone with the barista and he is muttering to himself and changing the radio to something punk and angry, and you are having an attack of the heart. Inside you, something overbalances. You tell yourself it's the caffeine. But really you expect, because you are you, that this is the moment of love's breaking off and drifting away and that after today you will reach your arm out after it forever. That you are going to lose everything you have ever loved.

But you sit there in the coffee shop and you feel such tenderness for the barista, who looks after all like Samuel, that little hump in the back of the neck, and something new is happening: love settles back in, but deeper.

This scares you. You had not known it was not, already, deep as it could go. This scares you more than loss, whose structures you have learned over time. Suddenly it occurs to you that Samuel may come to visit Baltimore someday and never leave. Suddenly when you think "I love you," you mean with your life. With the commitment of your life. Suddenly you start to feel things like, give your years to me and I will do the same. Suddenly our hearts pledged to each other means in this bigger adventure, not just this hotel room but this lifetime. Suddenly ownership is not some sexy game, Iz, suddenly I want to own him not as a collarbone is owned by a mouth but as a diamond is deeded from Nana's hand to mine upon her dying breath, I want him to be mine.

Love is a reverse birth. A monster animal that burrows ever deeper.

Samuel already knew about this shift, of course. My lover

that other species, he had this knowledge but he let it take me unprepared. I will prepare you, Isidore. You're lonely now but what if someday you are loved. Even as I say this, I am sorry. I know better than to plant hope in your heart. Love is nothing more than luck. Even if I get it, you may not. Even if I get it, I may not.

In all this I ignore the ghosts who hover at my shoulder, breathing down my neck. They have been here at the table all afternoon, trying to smell the coffee, fogging up the glass with their longing—these ghosts who are inside me, blackening my heart. Samuel, Samu-el: Your name has god inside it. I have two gods inside me too, myself and the children of that God of death, but you have never felt them. It's Iz who understands—

And so a monster animal that moves continues moving. I have thought so long of how to heal your brother, and the truth arrives too whole to be a story I made up: Your brother loves World War II. Your brother who is lonely. My Nana's story was never meant for Samuel, of course I couldn't tell it. Her story was a gift for my real love, my mirror-self, the loneliest man in the world.

The story, Iz, is she lost her brother and sister and village but survived somehow, in hiding walking down the street, her husband brought her chocolate. Later, she helped the Warsaw ghetto uprising. She never felt sure she had done the right thing; the men who took her orders survived in the dozens and not the hundreds. She felt guilty, she said in her living room, looking just over my shoulder. She had shortened people's intolerable lives, even by one day. Iz, you don't survive because you hope for better; you keep living because it is life. It is life and you have it and therefore you tend it. Maybe you hate it and it's just a fact and not a gift, maybe it's not beautiful at all and it's terrible suffering, still it is life and to have one more day of it is a holy thing.

So finally the story ends, with holiness's coda: I am in the line of death. I was one of those souls who never got to be made and therefore never should have been, causality runs only backward, the ghosts snuck in between my father and my mother years ago, they snuck in and for some reason this time they managed to survive the heat and blood and brightness of the living. I came out with my eyes open, my father says this. Something he interpreted as sharp and smart and curious. Something that was merely ready. I had been anticipating life for decades, watching jealous through the shower glass.

Maybe you are like me, Iz. We can have good lives we tend, but they will not be like the lives of the people on this side of the glass. We are ghost-made, the texture of loneliness.

I go now, Iz. It's not fair but even I leave you alone. I zip up my coat and tip the barista and I am going now to make a request of Samuel, my only addressee, my love my only law: What if you don't leave. Samuel, force the ghosts out of me. Seal the glass. Kill them finally. They were unmade and that was sad but they should stay that way. You stay. You tell them no, you tell them I don't need hope but I am the random lucky one, plucked out from the shower glass, I get to have it.

My father is old. Yours is older. I want them to meet us before they are gone.

LILITH
IN GOD'S HANDS

....

So God created mankind in his own image
. . . male and female he created them.
—Genesis 1:27

Do not pity me.

It's true my name is Lilith, known to history as the spurned first wife of Adam. But what story is as simple as a single sentence? He was no bargain, and let's not imagine he didn't suffer the loss of me. That woman Eve—you think she didn't have a first love, too?

Among us all, only Adam was unlucky enough never to see his love returned.

My poor, cruel, inelegant, lonely Adam.

....

So the story goes: I am Lilith, made of the same earth as Adam. Made of half his soul. Made of mud, bone, flesh, spirit, demon, word, story, stone, loss, longing, virtue, sin, forbearance.

Made of everything, except a rib.

The truth is, I don't remember my creation. I know only which tale I prefer: the one where God scooped up me and Adam in his big hands, in his right the clay that would be Adam and his left the clay that would be me. (Or vice versa—God has no heart, so why fight to be closest to it?) He clenched his fists, our torsos in his palms, and in the cracks between his knuckles Adam and I took shape: feet hooked on one side of his pinky, chests heaving up between the second and third fingers, chins craning from under the thumb.

I remember the feeling, squeeze and relief. Like birth.

Lilith is said to hate children—but only because I know they'll have to suffer. Some of them will be Lilith, some Eve, some Adam. Beloved, besotted, bereft. I had no mother, after all. Nor did Adam, nor Eve. Maternal love is natural or it is learned; we had no chance to learn it.

When it comes to hate: I hate no more than any mother hates her reckless idiots, flirting with the souls that will undo them.

………

We were both Adam, at first. Adam meaning earth. Meaning man. We had identical bodies. God called us by one name, and we came.

It is history's Adam who seeded the idea for "Lilith," in

the smoldering dark with his hand cupped over the rise of my hip. He sang to me, a wordless tune. It was a way of calling me, but it wasn't until later that I realized it could be my name: *La la.*

My favorite memory of Adam is there, right there, the buzz of his throat against my throat, his music thrumming in my ear. The leaves of Paradise soft beneath us both. His eyes like mine, his skin like mine, brown and rich and the same as the earth. I couldn't tell us apart sometimes, except I knew that he was singing and I must not be. *La la.*

"Who will we be when we're old?" I would say, talking idly over his song. "Will I become the one who sings to you?"

Love was different then, before choice. It was the same thing as hate. There was only one thing, and I called it that thing I feel for Adam, and he called it the same, and we had the gift of naming, and we named it love.

....

Of course, I didn't know that at the time. I talked myself hoarse to him. He sang me the lullabies that lovers sing— but that is only because we'd named ourselves lovers and the songs lullabies. We might have called them claws instead, and us foes. Then we'd have been foes clawing at each other, nonetheless inside the melody of an easy sleep on hallowed moonlit earth.

....

If I've stressed this name point strongly, it's because I am angry at God for offering the wrong kind of language. What we want are heartnouns, mindsongs, but we were given only throatnouns and mouthsongs to explain them to each other.

This is all to say that Adam and I loved each other, and I didn't know love meant a different thing to him than it did to me. I would not have asked God for a different Adam, not in a thousand thousand lifetimes. But he asked for a different Lilith.

....

Here there's been some misinterpretation. We speak now of rib, but the truth is breast. Both our chests once rose into the negative space of God's fist; now, Adam's went flat.

I like to think this was Adam's punishment. God could have chosen another spot of earth from which to forge this second partner, but he made Adam hurt for her instead. It is enough to make me trust God, for a moment. Then I remember:

As God was reaching into Adam, to rip him open and undo my twin's elegant body, I happened to walk into that bloody clearing with a handful of berries. In later years, I have discovered that I hate the chore of picking berries. I didn't know it then, because I was picking berries for Adam.

And there was blood, and there was God, his arm in the base of Adam's torn-out throat.

I screamed. I raced to kill God, to protect Adam, and in his fright God pressed a finger so deep inside Adam that he pushed his organs out between his legs. To this day, the womb replicates this accident: the embryo starts off female. This was the form of humankind, before God the sculptor blundered in his shame at knowing what he was doing and being caught by Lilith.

"I'm sorry," said God, "I'm so sorry," and he placed Eve on the earth that had made me.

Her body was slick with Adam's blood. The grisly scene looked grislier because I'd crushed the red berries in my fighting fists. In lonely years since, I've wondered whether I just wanted to be created again for Adam, too.

Adam's skin was pale and glistening redly. He staggered to his feet.

"Who said you could do this?" I asked God, trying to reach him, to beat him. God backed away. He pointed.

I followed his finger, around which Adam and I had gasped our first breaths. I stared into my Adam's muddy eyes, willing him not to have requested this other wife. He looked guiltily at the ground.

....

Much has been written of the Garden of Eden. Let me tell you something about Paradise: it is hellish as Satan's memory, when the person you love there doesn't love you.

....

Now, we invented new words: passion. Apathy. Desire. Disdain.

My hateful Adam adored her from the start, with all the depth of love that he could cull from his hollow chest. He trailed her through the paths of Eden. He never sang into my ear again.

But here's where the story gets interesting:

"La la," Eve called in the middle of the night.

"Hush," I told her. I tried to take pleasure in Paradise chirping its night song. "Hush, or Adam will hear."

"La la hush," she whispered, her breath buzzing at my throat. Her mouth traced down my ribcage and paused over the contained organs that Adam had lost to disdain me and desire her. Her eyes flicked like a serpent's up to mine.

"Lilith," she mumbled, her tongue between her teeth.

....

Adam found out soon enough, of course. There are no doors to close in a sprawling sun-soaked garden.

He hovered silently over us and I lay awake on my back, studying him. The sheen in his eyes, I had learned, did not mean a thing. It did not mean the same thing as the sheen in mine.

When he spoke, his lullaby voice was pitched low: "Do you truly hate me this much, Adam?"

Eve stirred sleepily against my breast. I stroked her forearm with my thumb. "That's your name now," I told him, shifting my gaze to a cloud that was covering the sun, avoiding the treacherous sympathy that would make me soft when I needed to be hard. "I don't want it anymore."

"Then what should I call you?"

We'd had lovely nights together, he and I, cradled on Eden's soil. We'd had to call each other nothing, when there was no one else to call.

"Witch?" he said. "Beast? Adulterer? Talk now if you've something to say. Tell me."

Beast. I felt a painful swelling start at the base of my throat. The story goes that Adam named them, the beasts of the field—but all it means is that he named me. When he stopped wanting to sing to me, he started speaking, and his words were ugly.

"I don't want to talk," I murmured, wanting him to ask again.

He pulled Eve out from under my arm. He said, "You love talking!"

Idiot boy. What I'd loved was talking to you.

....

Adam sent me away from Eden, and I left. It didn't matter where; two loves lost, no place could be a paradise for me anymore.

Eve watched me go. She watched my hips sway as I attempted a steady gait away; she watched my body sway as I couldn't manage it. She watched my cheeks burn as I looked back at Adam and saw that he was looking at her. She watched my knees buckle as I dropped one last time into the earth of Paradise, the closest I'd ever be to Adam again. She watched me press my face into the dirt. She may have watched me swallow a mouthful of soil. She watched me right myself and leave the garden, but this was a time before knowledge: she could not predict where I'd go.

Eve was a brilliant woman, made of the best of Adam and me, and now she was a broken woman. Her love went somewhere she couldn't follow, beyond the garden's gates—can you blame her for finding the forbidden fruit that very hour, and banishing herself where she might find me?

Brilliant, broken, brazen, brave. These are words that Eve and I made up together. These are our words, women's words, words we chose for the beginning of a wandering world.

. . . .

The story that comes next has been rewritten. Of course it's been rewritten; Eve is first woman because she was first mother, that's all. It is her sons and theirs who wrote the story.

Let me tell you: Eve didn't care if Adam ate the fruit. She left it in the sun to rot. She was already halfway to the garden's gate when he came running, spitting apple seeds.

I'm told that she did not look back to greet him.

. . . .

Do not pity me, though I am Lilith, the scorned first wife of Adam. I have had my years for pity. I have taken the name given by the woman willing to take me. I have not won, but I have not lost. I have grown content. I worry sometimes that my heart is turning cold, from lack of someone to give myself to, but then Eve wanders into me and I pour out as much love as I can before she leaves. I redefine love by the day, the moment, the place I'm at in the story I'm telling. God sometimes visits, to apologize. I send him away. It is not so bad.

A man's word, pity. If you must use it, then pity Adam, who could not learn to love what loved him: boneless Adam, broken Adam, Adam of the earth, Adam singing, Adam of the space inside God's hands.

TO LOSE
EVERYTHING
I HAVE EVER LOVED

. . . .

He does it. Samuel, finally, he can't live without me.

How he makes it to me isn't clean. He picked his wife, by not-picking. He kept on saying maybe and saying maybe until Anne found my footsteps in the snow and made him swear never to talk to me again. When it came to her, he said okay. He swore. When it comes to me, he lasts a week shy of a year. My Friend and I are at the bar that has replaced our coffee shop, drinking old-fashioneds because I'm mad that I have nowhere else to be and she's mad that she and alive new husband aren't pregnant yet. My phone buzzes on the table. My Friend and I both look: Samuel's name on the screen.

God I have missed his name on the screen.

I unlock the text, expecting an apology. Instead I find a photo of his penis. "Are you kidding me," says my Friend. "Tell him to fuck off." But I'm not offended. How I have missed his penis. The only penis I have ever loved, the only one I ever studied with enough interest to memorize. The only one I could describe the feeling of, lip and curve. I look at it on the screen until my Friend gives a loud sigh.

"Tell him you're out drinking with somebody else, then," she says. "At least tell him that."

I meet her halfway. *I'm sorry*, I text, *was this intended for your other mistress?*

No, he answers. *Sorry that was weird. I've been thinking of you, Dinah. Baby.*

Maybe I've been beaten down too long. Being unloved, it does strange things to you. You take what you can get. You know you should have better and that better doesn't come your way. I've tried manifesting something better, I get nowhere. I remember what my Nana Itta used to say, looking at old photographs of the dead in her living room: Your grandpa never brought me down, he always brought me up. I want to rise in love, too, I know that's what love should do—but I can't forever live as if what should be, will be. As if what should be, is.

So my Friend orders a third drink, and sits back, and Samuel and I text. He grows fervid, obsessed, wild, desperate. His fantasies grow more carnal, move from the flesh to the fluid. He needs to touch me again, he has to be inside me again. At strategic moments I say, *Yes I need you too, Yes we need this, Birdbaby what will we do about it?*

I am careful to say "we," careful to show nothing falls too squarely at his feet, neither blame nor onus to act. He tells me he got a new job, as a cartoonist for a paper in New Hampshire. An impossible job in this day and age. An anachronism of a job. Isn't he the luckiest? He tells me they are packing their Boston apartment. Yes, right now. Anne is in the bedroom nestling their high school yearbooks into boxes, and he's thinking it's now or never. They can unpack again in separate apartments. He is going to tell her so.

"See?" I say to my Friend, holding out the phone with his text.

"You're shaking," says my Friend.

I don't know how many cocktails I've had at this point. Never mind, says my Friend, that now or never came for me a year ago. She leans forward and she must be a drink or two ahead of me. "Ask him to do it now," she tells me, go ahead, she doesn't have a kid at home or anything, she'll wait.

So I ask if he might have a talk with the wife right now. He doesn't answer for so long that our waitress's shift ends and she closes us out and my Friend starts a tab with the bartender. Then he says he did it. Ten years after marrying his wife, two weeks after selling their condo in Boston and taking her out to dinner when she quit her job, one week before moving her to their new home in New Hampshire for his new job in New Hampshire, he tells her for the first time that he's doubting the relationship. He wants to take a break.

I don't even have the time to close my jaw before he texts again. The wife has said no to a break. Of course. She's in it too deep with him now, she'd rather him than no one, I understand her. My sister. We both know something is better than nothing, when it comes to love. We both know the alternative to worse-something might not be better-something. We both know people like my Friend seem not to think this, or claim not to. They seem to think nothing is better than bad-something. Anne and I can't live the one life we each have according to the wisdom of other people.

So Anne says no to a break. He can't quite bring himself to say well then, he wants a divorce—and I feel the extremely, unfairly long tether of my patience snap. I almost throw the phone. *Fuck it*, I text him, *I'm sick of asking when, I'm getting drunk with an ex.* "You're right," I tell my Friend. "I'm an idiot."

"You're not an idiot for hoping," she says, but she's slurring. My father used to call her in the psych ward, years ago when she was the crazy one, with an ex who'd killed himself. My father used to talk to her until she was ready to hang up. All I do is put her in a cab and kiss her on the forehead and text alive new husband that she's on her way. Then I walk home, curl up on my side in bed, and have a talk with Nana, who is dead. "Nana," I say. "He's never coming back." I want her to say something I'm unable to invent for her, something ancient and wise. But she doesn't say anything. The unmade ghosts start whispering in my ear. *No one is coming for you*, they say. *It can happen, you know. Nobody came for us.*

They're vibrating in my skull. I tap my sinuses to try and

shake them out. But then I realize the vibration isn't them; it isn't even the beginnings of a hangover; it's my phone, buzzing on my pillow.

Are you sleeping with him? Samuel has texted.

With who? I almost write, but I see my own text above his. An ex, I'd said. A fiction. I don't reply, because what could I say? My sex is shaped like Samuel, I told him this long ago at the start of our affair and it's true, God help me. There is no one else. But he keeps texting, cycling himself through wrong stories—*It's fine if you're sleeping with him, You're allowed but I have to know, Please tell me you're not fucking him, Holy shit you're fucking him*—to which I do not respond. I watch the texts roll in with a sort of detached interest in the story he's weaving for my life. I half-wish that I really were doing the things he imagines. Pulling some man into my bed. The texts keep coming, and just as I am thinking that he has truly lost the plot, unmoored from the realities of my world and finding endless evidence for the fantasies of his, he breaks his escalating panic with a text that says, *I'm talking to her now.* And early that morning, after I'm already sleeping, I wake to a phone call and he says, "I'm yours."

It is a real effort of will, of sheer memory, to say the first words I have always planned: "I promise to take care of Iz."

. . . .

So I am with him. Finally: love. The only thing I've always wanted. The only thing I thought I'd never get. I leave

Baltimore for him, say goodbye to my Friend in the bar, move with him into a duplex in Portsmouth, next door to a couple in their sixties who play the violin together every night. We have a desk for my writing on the first floor and a table for his drawing in the basement. I sleep beside him in a bed that I paid half of, I have a side of the bed. I sing him lullabies I adapt, *Hush little bird* and *Good night sweet bird good night*. Badah da da da dum, he sings back. He is a body and, even more, he is Samuel's body, the collar-bone as hollow as a sparrow's, the mouth that laughed when I climbed onto him that first night in the B&B with my heart wild and my thighs spread.

And yet.

After all the frenzy of packing and moving and adding *Live free or die* to my license plate, I am standing in the kitchen on our first Friday night in our new condo, preheating the oven. The violins next door are keeling. Samuel is humming a little tune beside me at the stove, bopping his hip into mine, brining a chicken. Everything I ever wanted. Here I am. I wait to feel the way my Friend must have felt all these years, every time she went home to her husband on the couch: a song in my heart that is the knowledge that I have a man to cook with, to talk to, to wake in the night if I think I'm having an aneurism. To run away with, if the government should turn against us.

I listen for that song. I really do.

But my heart isn't singing. It's thumping like it's caffein-ated, talking like a ghost. It says he's done the coming-to-me in the worst way. After Anne gave up her house and job and friends for him, is when he left her. Even though he had months and years to do it in before. He already knew he was wanting to go, and yet he let her stay so long, preheating his oven.

And he has done it in the worst way in another way. He spent a year not-choosing me before he chose me. He left me to suffer, unwanted, straining to hear Nana's dead-voice willing me out of the bed I'd bought alone. For this sin he should have come back crawling. Begging my forgiveness. Instead he has come back proclaiming his own bravery, expecting to be praised. Proclaiming his own woundedness, expecting to be soothed. Maybe I have enabled this. The way I got him back was by not-emphasizing how much penance he would owe me. I knew, instinctively, that he would not return for that.

So while I'm put in charge of the chicken because he has to run to the basement, there's a river system growing in his mind, I sneak downstairs. In the basement he is hunched over his new drawing table, sketching a complicated web of canals. His tongue between his lips. That little hump at the base of his neck. I wonder where the maps inside his head come from. I wonder why he can draw imaginary transit systems with such intricacy, but couldn't find a path to get to me while I still thought he'd never give me up.

He must sense me in the doorway. He looks up, sees me. Smiles. Tells me to come over here, come kiss him on the forehead, come love him for being the mapmaker and mine.

I almost say: Why did it take you so long?

I go over. I kiss him. I wonder if anyone is coming to save me. I remember my neighbors from when I was growing up, the night the old woman screamed across the fences between yards that her husband had fallen. My cousins and I had been at home alone, and we hid under the window so we wouldn't have to help.

....

Back when I only wanted him, I was full of futures. How I would hold him every night, how I would thrill to be the woman of the mapmaker, how I would stand in adoration in the doorway of his drawing room. Now that I have him, I am full of looking-backward. I remember a certain afternoon in Massachusetts, years ago. He was still with Anne. I was spending a month up north to assuage his fears about leaving her, hoping if I showed him the goodness of my love at close range he would stop being afraid. By night I wandered around Boston, no one to talk to, a walking wannabe love story, a monologue in my head that kept losing the me of things. *You*, my whole world was an address to a you who wasn't there to answer. I didn't believe in the rules of civility back then, but had not yet learned to make my own rules in their stead. I didn't know that all I had to do was shut up about how sad he made me and go fuck an ex.

By day, when he could get away, we would meet in the Boston Common. One afternoon early in the visit, I got mad at him on a park bench. For no reason, for reading too long without looking up at me. And right there in the first week of the long month we'd planned together, I told him he'd missed his chance with me, he'd been too slow and assumed I'd wait too long. He had cried. Said he loved me and that we were just starting this adventure that was going to make him strong, why was I beating him down when he was being brave?

That night, I lay alone on the pullout couch of the sublet he had found me for the month, while he was home in bed with Anne and their dog. I looked up at the ceiling of my new bedroom, missing Nana, willing her to appear to me like Emma Thompson through the ceiling. I thought, What inside my heart is structured wrong? There on the bench had been this man who loved me, a man with a collarbone hollow like a bird's. The only love I may ever know in my life, and I closed my heart to him.

I remember feeling the ghosts all over me in bed. Clawing at my pelvis. I tried to ignore them. I tried to picture Nana who'd escaped the curse of death in Poland long ago, Nana whose children and grandchildren were real, here on earth, and not ghosts on the other side of the glass wall that separated the living from the dead. I thought not of Nana's husband who always brought her up, but of my own curdling heart that would have made him turn away. I longed for Samuel that night. I texted him endless times: *I'm sorry, You've probably given up on me, I must be jetlagged, Give me another chance.* And he said, *We'll do better tomorrow,* and it was a balm I held all sleepless night as I promised myself that every time I saw him after that I'd love him with the force of my life.

....

I call my cousin. Nana, would Nana be happy, I have a partner, maybe we'll make children.

Though Samuel says he's not sure he wants children, and the truth is we've had so much unprotected sex that I've started to suspect that either he's infertile, or I am. Lately too I've thought of Anne, how they never even had a scare, and I've wondered if he got a secret vasectomy years ago.

"I'm not sure it's me he loves," I say. "He loves this person who managed to trick him, by accident then on purpose, that she slept with an ex-boyfriend who doesn't exist. I don't have an ex-boyfriend. Doesn't he remember? This can't be healthy."

"Who says love is healthy," says my cousin. Her brother has been married for years now, to a Methodist who gives us cash for Christmas. In the meantime, she's still adding man after man to her list. "Love is fire, passion, insanity. Aren't you the one who's read all the books? The passion love is never civil or respectful. All our Western pop-psych crap just says that to contain us, Dinah. They just want us not-howling."

....

Samuel and I join his new colleagues on a bar crawl in Portsmouth. I know two people in the biergarten of the second place, to everyone's surprise, friends of mine from Baltimore who hadn't been a couple when I knew them but are a couple now. They are on vacation for their anniversary. Leaf peeping, they say. Samuel is nervous about the guys from editorial, and I am trying to prove that life with me is less stressful than life with Anne, so I try to get him a cigarette. "Do you have an extra one of those?" I say, when my friend pulls out his pack. My friend looks at me stupidly until the phrase *Can I bum one* rises in my mind, and Samuel says, "She's asking for me."

I smoke the cigarette fresh from Samuel's lips, to demonstrate that we are together. When the two men start talking about cigars or something, the girl says, "Your boyfriend's nice." I am a little drunk and a little high on cigarettes I don't normally smoke. I say, "After all these years of being single, I think I'm bad at being someone's girlfriend."

I feel I've spoken the truest, ugliest secret of my heart. The curdled thing in the pit of me, turning love away right when I've cajoled it to my park bench.

She says—she has red lips perfectly outlined, she knew me during the years I was alone—"I'm sure that isn't true."

And it *isn't* true; I'd gotten upset at Samuel at the previous bar, the one full of his people and not mine, because of how very much of our relationship is full of his things and not mine. I want to explain this to the girl. I may have overpromised, I almost say, back when he had a wife and I couldn't have him. When you're pushing against a brick wall, push as hard as you want and it won't budge. But when it gives way. Maybe you find, if you keep pushing that hard, you fall over.

The girl takes a second cigarette from her boyfriend's pocket. Samuel holds the lighter in front of her lips. He stays outside smoking longer than I expect him to. Samuel likes red lipstick, I know this about him. When we get home, he goes to his drawing table still flicking the lighter in his hand. I shower to get rid of the smoke in my hair. I smell cigarettes washing down the drain, and I think about the fact that, when a healthy body gets cancer, it's more prepared to fight than an already unhealthy body. I wasn't healthy when it came to love, before him, so maybe I'm too weak to fight the battles this relationship will take.

My Friend doubts the veracity of this medical analogy. She says so on our weekly brunch-time videocall. A marathoner's body, more proficient at regenerating cells, makes cancer at a rate that far outstrips a couch potato's. She insists on this. Her aunt smoked a pack of cigarettes a day and barely left her recliner and lived to ninety-seven.

My great-aunt and -uncle milked cows in a field four miles from their home, and got killed by a bullet to the back of their extremely healthy heads.

....

Two months, or six. I forget to care about his collarbone. His dreams of drowning, the raised vein on his bicep whose path I have memorized. I forget to reiterate our little mythologies. That our souls knew each other back when souls were clustered in the center of the universe, before they got split into a hundred billion bodies. That ours have spent millennia trying to hold hands. That the depression under our noses is where the face knits together in the womb, and you can see an angel's kiss right at the seam, and the equivalent seam of his scrotum has a sudden side-track up the left ball because his angel sneezed.

One day I am palming him there—a smaller form of sex has endured between us, though I'm not sure I would call it sacred anymore—and he says, "Achoo." And I stare at him, blank-eyed, for so long that I can watch some of his hope die in his eyes.

It does make me sad. But not sad enough to say anything. I am thinking of the bar in Baltimore that I've given up to be here with him, wondering if even now he's texting someone on the side.

He swears he'd never do that to me. I'm not sure I believe him.

"Yeah right," my Friend says over video brunch, where she is noticeably not-drinking.

"Fine," I say, "I'm sure I don't believe him."

"So what will you do about it?" she says.

Samuel would want me to say, Nothing, what's done is done, he's hurt me as he has and I've chosen him anyway. I can't fight the past into changing, it's no one's fault, I have cultivated in myself Zen and calm from a long lineage of anxiety and fear.

I can't say it. My Friend lets the silence sit. Then she takes a deep breath and says, "When I was in the institution, I made friends with a bunch of suicidal people."

Alive new husband knows her as a sales manager who orders nonstick cookware; she rarely talks about her time in the institution.

"Dumb idea," she says, "putting someone who thinks suicide makes sense in a roomful of people who agree. It's the psychologists who start to seem out of their minds then. They used to give us assignments. Make a case for life to God, they said. Trust us, life makes sense, choosing life makes sense, fighting for life makes sense. Tell God why. And you know, Dinah, none of us agreed. We couldn't make the case, we laughed at them. They must have felt like the crazy ones. They must not have believed in what they were saying."

She takes a sip of tea.

"But they said it anyway. You hear me, Dinah? They said it anyway."

....

I start to think it has all been a problem of genre. During those years I spent loving a man who wasn't mine, I thought I was living a romance, or maybe a tragedy. My Friend tried to get me to see it as a comedy. In fact it was a horror story.

So I plan to write a new essay, my first in this period of Samuel's return to me. This time I will be clear-eyed. Even still I can't help hoping that it might be joy, a celebration, a letting-out of breath. But what pours out of me is not an essay at all; it's more like a dream, about a man who runs away from the woman who loves him and applies for a mission to Mars.

I read it with a knowing heart. Though it's a flight story, it isn't my bird Samuel at the center of it. It's a not-enough-yet story, I can feel this, full of old longing.

....

One night, Samuel puts on a peacoat and I put on low heels and red lipstick and we go to dinner to introduce me to his family.

Samuel's face is a younger version of his parents' faces. I greet them, these maps of his future. I hug his mother, I kiss his father on the cheek, everybody cedes the head of the table to the patriarch. Samuel's father is old, but smart like his son, prickly and fun to argue with. He is a conservationist who is the reason there was a river under the bridge where I first met Samuel years ago. He is his son's hero. But even at ninety, he glances sidelong at the waitress and I catch his wife seeing, then ignoring his gaze. I pity her. Suddenly, strangely, I also pity Anne. I order a soup instead of salad feeling a weird, first gratitude toward Anne, for having put up with Samuel for so long; and a weird, first guilt, for having stolen from her someone I don't want to keep forever after so short a time.

I feel the warm flush of this pity and gratitude and guilt

rising in my cheeks. I try to look in-love. I distract myself by fiddling with my phone. Samuel's mother smiles at me. I smile back. Samuel, for his part, notices my flush and puts his arm around my waist at the table. I haven't brought my own father, because I haven't wanted him to see exactly this: I, whether like or not-like Samuel's mother and ex-wife, have found out how to keep my partner's eye on me. It's a formula, so simple that sometimes in the shower pulling hair between my fingers it makes me cry. Tease him with my words but deny him my body until he's good. Make it a sexy game, goodness and ownership, but tie the game to looking my way instead of somebody else's. Intimate with blushes and flustered looks that I may or may not have just received a text from a vague ex I never name.

This is what I've done right now, by accident. I watch Samuel's eyes not only slide back from the waitress to me, but snap back. The version of him I fell in love with taught me about sin and sacredness. That man was playing together with me on a holy plane. This one is threatened by an ex who doesn't exist. I dip my cloth napkin into my ice water and blot my forehead. The little lies it takes to keep him are so easy, so effective. I can tell him I'm touching my wet hot anything while I'm really doing the dishes. He tells me stories in return. Like the one he is telling now, holding court at the table, in which I am the love of his life, tender and carnal, mapmaking and servile and sweet. It was always going to be me, bound to be me, he was destined to wind up here in Portsmouth humming to the neighbors' violin.

Destined to be asking, "Honey, should we get the mahogany couch frame, or the walnut?"

Who is he talking to, I wonder. Who does he think he's talking to. I'm the girl who believed she inherited aloneness from her Nana's ghosts, the girl who promised first thing to take care of Samuel's brother, because I thought I understood that lonely man in ways he never could.

I didn't, by the way. Understand Isidore. Understand anything. I meet Iz too here at the restaurant, where he doesn't order a thing. I want to like him. He nods at me and sits on Samuel's other side and tells me about the drive, but he doesn't look me in the eye. Maybe he thinks I am a member of the well-loved. Maybe, almost, I am. He folds his napkin into shapes in a way that seems animated, maybe happy. He has the same guffaw as his brother. Maybe he has it right, keeping himself to himself. I had nothing to teach him, of course. Maybe I could have learned from him. Or maybe no one learns from anyone, such hubris. All those sitcom wives already told me: love isn't so great. Sure, the first blush is a trip. After that it's a fall. The kind that breaks your neck.

On the screen of his watch, Samuel shows Iz the latest stats from the Patriots game. Their father leans in to see, too. The mother and I pull their ties out of their soups. Iz is the only one who didn't choose this situation for himself, I think, the only one who's sitting here out of pure biology, which I respect. Which I like.

Nana's voice in my ear: "You don't have to like him, Dinah. The innocent victim is not the moral good, though the oppressor is the moral bad. I'm not good, necessarily, just because I lost my world."

"But Nana, this is not right," I think.

"No," I can almost hear her saying, "my Dinah, this Samuel is not the man I want for you. You know this, have always known this."

Samuel runs his pinky finger up my thigh under the table. An old game between us, batting flirtation back and forth in public, a holdover from when our love had to exist in secret under tables. I push him off. Not in front of Iz, I try to tell him with my eyes. But Samuel never understood the contours of loneliness, how it makes other people's thigh-touching look exquisite and impossible. He is with me and still he doesn't know. He is with me and so he doesn't know.

I nod and smile through it all: the drive home that night, to the dog bed in the living room for the dog his ex-wife kept. The obsession over the next few weeks with buying a new couch, with anchoring in one place even as he can't stop looking at the waitress. The desire over the next few months to go on more vacations of the kind where he started an affair with me, to leave me at home with his furniture.

....

But it's him or nothing, for this lifetime.

"Maybe so," says my Friend on the phone, in an honest mood. "Surely not," says my Friend, in a platitudinous one. She has had a miscarriage that I am struggling to find my sympathy for. I am pretty convinced by now, after count-less sex at every possible time of month, that Samuel's angel sneeze is a vasectomy scar, though he insists he has no idea what I'm talking about.

"Having nothing is better than having a man whose very testicles you don't trust," says my Friend.

"I know," I say, testing it out. Feeling a surge of truth and power in it. Knowing even so that this power is only the re-vokable privilege of having. Without him I will look back and forgive him everything, so he looked at the waitress, so it took some manufactured jealousy to get to him, he came home every night and tucked the quilt around my feet. It is only when I have him that I can imagine I'd be gladder having lost him.

This, of course, is my problem. Nana's ghosts are clam-bering inside me, dumb dead unmade, they still think any-body living is a prize.

....

The incels have kept writing. All this time. Okay, I want to tell them, you're right, life is often terrible, lonely, it isn't fair, it isn't bearable, somebody should pay. You prophesize your own aloneness, it comes true. Maybe you create this truth. Or maybe you're simply an excellent prophet.

But you're wrong, I want to tell them. The one who needs to pay—it isn't me.

....

So, though I am sick at heart and was before I met him, I am going to leave him. I will have missed my chance to continue Nana's line, by then. I will be the reason all my bad-ghost premonitions have come true. In the meantime I am stroking his hair, knowing he doesn't repay she who strokes him, collecting being-loved within me for a someday. Someday I'll be so full of the strength of having had him that I can coast on it for years after I don't.

My Friend takes to calling when she's walking down in Baltimore, when she doesn't have anything to say. I take to walking in New Hampshire holding her on the phone. Sometimes one of us talks; sometimes neither of us does. In one of these silences, I tell her: There was a piece of me, I can admit it now, who when he said *I'm yours*, thought: fuck. This is how I'll end up childless, this is the reason my father won't have grandkids, this is the story my cousins' children will hear of why I'm alone. This is how my Nana's unmade ghosts come claim me, not in loneliness but in the Trojan horse of love.

My Friend has to clear her throat a few times to find her voice. Then she says that this is the condition of women, to be constantly placating and pretending to the ferocity of men. "Why do you think women call their man to kill a mouse," she says, "when we can deliver dead babies into toilet bowls and barely even scream."

"You screamed?" I say.

"No," she says. "Only out loud."

....

After my Friend and I hang up, I walk for a while longer in the cold. It's been minutes or maybe hours, but I am still holding the phone to my ear. I am going to lose everything I have ever loved: I am speaking these words to myself, over and over, walking around and around my block, waiting to hear the violins calling me home.

I am going to lose everything I have ever loved. I am going to choose to, someday. For so long I'd been sick of finding yet new ways to write *He left me,* for so long I believed if love ever came my way I'd be incapable of falling out of it, I'd be unlike those ungrateful others who married their high school sweethearts—and even so. Even so having is worse than getting. So I'm going to have to be brave. I'm going to decide to lose the only thing I ever wanted. The question is when.

The sun sets early in New Hampshire, and any trace of warmth with it. Finally, full with my mantra, I go home. Samuel claps his phone shut as soon as I walk in the door. Too fast, maybe? I consider asking to see the screen. Choose not to start a fight, or not to verbalize the fight that he's already started. I say hi, brave love, sweet bird. My own voice sounds flat to me. I lie down on the walnut couch that half-belongs to him. He lies down next to me, says my hands are freezing, wraps my body in his body, chest to chest, breath back and forth between my mouth and his. Yes, it feels better to be held than not-held. No, today is not the day I leave him. Not yet. I grew up hiding under the window, knowing any neighbor will pick up a gun against any neighbor and shoot them in the back of the head. It never surprised me, when people couldn't love each other. It was more surprising when they could. Even for a year. Even for a day. Even for an hour, eye to eye, holding on, the man with the hollow collarbone that used to drive me to my knees.

TO DO WITH
THE BODY

....

I showed up at the Museum of Period Clothes dressed like a Revolutionary bayonetsman, like an idiot. All around me framed in glass were dresses hard with blood.

Normally I could have laughed off my mistake, but just then I was at the stage of heartbreak when failing to put on fitted sheets the right way could land me crying at the foot of the bed with the comforter in a heap. In that stage I never did anything but think of you. Get out of here, my roommate had said that morning when I tried to describe the eggs you used to crack for breakfast, go get dressed, go to a museum, come back when you can talk about anything else.

So there I stood in the entryway of red-brown skirts, holding a steak knife taped to a broomstick, confronting a sign that said: HOW MUCH BLOOD HAVE YOU LET?

That was something else to talk about. I calculated. I was thirty-three, and had had 234 periods in my life. That's 1,170 days of bleeding. Three full years of blood.

I thought that might interest you. I called you up. I was surprised that you answered. You had said you wouldn't answer me anymore, because the woman you loved had told you that you couldn't answer me anymore, but I always did suspect that she only had half a hold on you. Even "no" you couldn't follow through with, when it came to me.

You agreed to meet me at the Museum of Period Clothes. You didn't bother asking why there, though I'd prepared a reason. You were an important period, to me. You would not have pushed me further.

When you arrived, my eyes were a bayonet straight to my gut. You looked like you. Because I was in the middle of losing you—as I will always be in the middle of losing you; it's too far in to be the beginning but it will never end—I'd thought you might look different. I'd worn a costume that went back in time 250 years. I thought perhaps the loss of me might have disjointed your chronology too, that you'd be dressed up like a space robot or a fig leaf, but you were wearing blue jeans and a red T-shirt and you stained my whole heart purple.

"Hello," you said, as if you could say any old thing, Goodbye or Nice morning or Wow you're alive. At least you didn't say how are you.

"Come walk," I said.

I chose the first room to our left. In sealed glass fishbowls were the old rags women in the Bible used to sit on, then pads with and without wings, cotton and linen, belts and straps, adhesive and Velcro, tampons and applicators. I wanted to stay there, all that absorption, but you said let's check out the Hall of What's Been Ruined: men's windbreakers, futilely tied around women's waists. Wedding dresses, of course. An underground storage unit full of underwear, pajama pants, sheets and stockings, couches and desk chairs and drivers' seats and mattresses and stairwell banisters.

HOW DOES IT MAKE YOU FEEL? read the signs on thin metallic music stands every few feet. There were little white index cards with little red crayons to draw your feelings. There were understanding female docents posted in the doorways to discuss your feelings.

Here is how it made me feel: Come back.

Because even when I used to have you, I never had you completely. You were always half with her. Even there, in that Museum that day you came half back to me: I nudged you to answer how does it make you feel, but you were texting someone, laughing to yourself. On your screen it said Eva. How is a Revolutionary bayonetsman supposed to deal with a betrayal via text. For months when I'd been boring my roommate to death over you, you were having her and laughing. Something about this fact was so evil that I wanted to do evil in response. What merely minor depravity could have possibly matched yours.

It struck me that the Museum of Period Clothes would be the perfect place to kill someone. There would be too much blood elsewhere to notice. To kill, specifically, a man. To comment upon the bleeding of violence and accident—the skinned knee, the guillotine, the bullet, the bayonet—versus the bleeding of nature.

I grabbed you by the back of the head and held the steak knife to your throat. I looked up at the understanding docent, murderously. She smiled back at me. She had blood between the pantlegs of her uniform. I waited to see what you would say. You'd been a poet when I knew you, I'd been a storyteller, you used to make such wonders emerge from that bloody throat.

Gurgle, is what you said. I'd pressed too hard to hear your last words, already. I planned to press harder, but at the last minute I changed my mind and plunged the knife into your abdomen, where you had a birthmark shaped like a tidal wave, which I used to love to kiss. Back then when I kissed that wave I never wanted to stop talking to you. You made my brain move in ways I didn't know it could, like an elbow bending backward. Without you, I could never find the way to make the muscle go. When we were together I wanted your mind. I was so greedy. I wanted your brain and your eyeballs. I wanted to live like a planet in constant revolution around you. I wanted to see myself through your eyes, because before you chose her instead of me, you used to make me feel so beautiful I glowed. God, how I loved you.

As much, I gathered, as you loved her.

You bled out at my feet. Art is a scream, you told me once. You were a thief of an artist; when you left me you stole all my words, you wrote poems with the lines I'd wanted to use, you ate the whole dictionary. Poetry, you told me. It's a way of screaming.

Your face was frozen in a look of Lily-why. Your blood was deep red over where I guess your wave had been. The understanding docent looked away. The other Museum visitors looked at me in appreciation. My eighteenth-century costume must have appeared all the more authentic for your blood. The Museum closed. The night guards didn't kick me out. You were so lovely that I looked at you all night. I looked at you until I didn't know who you were. Then I left. I didn't ask what they planned to do with the body.

. . . .

Years later, I go back. You are still there. It is a shock to see you, all in person. You are so different from the way my fuzzy love-brain has recorded you: your hairline is more receded, your beard is frizzier, your teeth are yellower and the two in front hyperextend, your tongue is more rolled backward down your throat, your hands are larger, the gash in your abdomen is closer to the pubic bone, your jeans are lighter and your blood is darker. I love you so much I could almost un-kill you.

But only almost. Because the good news is, during these long years I have missed you as much as I would have if I'd never left you in the Museum—but she has also had to miss you, which has made me happy. KNOW THYSELF, read the signs over the ovulation trackers in the lobby. Myself knew how you made me feel like the most beautiful human thing on the planet after just a few months in your bed, and could not have stood the thought of her walking around the world feeling beautiful like that. Sometimes I have wondered if I should have killed her instead of you, but then you would have found someone else to make beautiful and I would have had to kill that one, too, in an endless cycle.

I am examining your eyelashes when I feel something heavy drop between my legs. I go to the bathroom—what did I expect, they overcharge me for a Museum-brand tampon and I wasn't allowed to bring my own, they checked my bag as if for popcorn at the movies—and when I come back, there is a woman beside you whose white slacks are so deeply scarlet I think she, too, must be dead. But I look at her eyes and they are all movement: she is watching your body with such heart-smashed momma-love that I know she must be the girl you chose instead of me.

I pretend not to know anything about her. I pretend not to know you, even. You are one of the only men in the Museum. Women come to you in droves. I pretend to just be one of them. I hope the momma-love in my eyes will not give me away.

"Are you the docent?" I say.

She shows me a nametag pinned to her blazer, which says Docent Flores. She says, "But only for this one."

I am jealous. Why didn't I think of becoming your docent? If I'd envisioned such displays of adoration for you, then maybe you'd have picked me and been my guest to somebody else's murder, instead of Exhibit A.

"It's a good piece," I say, walking around you, leaning in close to your groin, unseeable through the zipper and the coagulated blood. "Who's the artist?"

She looks at me funny. She says, "I am."

Bitch.

She goes on, "He hurt me so bad I had to kill him."

The murder in her voice is so strong that I wonder for a second if she didn't kill you, after all.

"Cheater?" I say.

She shakes her head. "He loved somebody else," she says. "Every moment I had him he was half going away."

I feel so soul-seen I could die. Oh my sister, I want to say.

"I like him better like this," she says, and her voice changes, all tender and sweet. She pats the hilt of the knife as if to drive it in a fraction deeper. "Like this I have him all the way. I can look at him as long as I want to, and he never says stop."

Who did you belong to, then? I want to say to you.

I decide that I will be your docent, too. I apply. I check the box that says I am willing to collect my menstrual blood for the bonsai garden on the second floor. On my first day of work, I walk in and receive my name tag and station myself in one corner of your room, and she stations herself in the other.

"Docent Flores," I say.

"Docent Sommers," she says.

Then we go silent, and that's it for us for months. We walk around you, we admonish the women who stand too close, we say no touching, we usher visitors to the gallery of red tissue-paper collages and plasma Rorschachs, we push your locks of hair behind your ear, we rearrange the baby's breath we have taken to putting in your shirt pocket, we make little comments to each other when the silence goes too long, Cold out there, Forget the back lot today there's a protest, Did you hear the docent on the second floor got fired, I knew someone was sleeping with security, those guys take lunches three hours long. We never talk about the exhibit. But I notice sometimes, when I come back from my lunch break, that she makes a quick step toward the wall like she's been speaking in your ear. And I bet she sometimes notices, when she comes back from her lunch break, that I have been pressing my palm to the hard place on your chest where your heart used to beat, tapping my heel in slow thuds on the marble floor.

Three cycles of bleeding after I start work, the security guard from the second floor comes downstairs to say he is moving you up. You are no longer What's Been Ruined, I'm informed. From now on, you will be a scarecrow for the bonsai. The guard crouches in front of you and wraps his big strong arms around your deflated calves. I rush toward you in the center of the room; another pair of hands is already wrapped around your chest; as one, Docent Flores and I say, "No!" and yank you away.

"You don't know what we do with him down here," I tell the guard.

"You're just the bonsai guy," she says. "Get out."

The guard leaves. She and I straighten the cuffs of your jeans. We are both at your feet when she reaches up and touches your chest and says, "He seems sad." She looks me in the eye. "Do you think he's sad?"

I don't know what it was about that guard, why he made her break our silence on the subject of you, but I am glad he did, because this morning I peeked into my roommate's bedroom and realized that his bed was gone. He moved out in January, read the note on the floor. I'd been alone all winter and hadn't even known it.

"Sad?" I say. She is wearing a decorative brooch on her lapel today, though we aren't supposed to wear anything other than our uniforms. The brooch is shaped like a tidal wave.

"A little longing," she says. "Like he wishes he could be alive."

I am thinking that you look rather happy today to be dead and cared for, but I don't tell her. I gaze at you, I address you for the first time in her presence, I say, "Do you miss being alive to witness blood?"

You don't answer, of course. You are still dead, just like yesterday. Me, I have to remake my decisions every day—there is no such thing as decision-making, only decision-remaking, yes okay today I'm glad I killed you—but you don't ever question. Every day, again, dead.

It must be something in the way I'm looking at you. We catch each other with the same expression in our eyes. She says, "You're Lily, aren't you."

She doesn't seem angry. I make a decision. I say, "You must be Eva."

Though we have worked together for six months, we shake hands.

"You're beautiful," I say, meaning it.

She tells me, "You are too."

It is midway through my lunch break, twenty minutes until hers. We tell each other, why not eat together. We smile. We tell your body: This does not concern you.

....

Eva and I eat lunch together whenever we're at work. We help each other sneak in the cheap tampons. She finds me a one-bedroom in her building, and I move. We talk about you, what you used to do and say, the way you used to kiss with just the slightest bite to the lower lip, how you would leap onto our backs without civility when we were sleeping, how you laughed with the longest eyelashes in the world. I tell her that you smell metallic in a different way than the rest of the Museum, the iron of chainmail and warriors. I ask if she agrees and she says yes, huh, you know, she really does. "I didn't actually make him," she says to me then, honest because we are friends, so I say, "I wonder who did."

She's seen me carve a roast beef sandwich; I know she knows it's my knife in your stomach. She nods. She says, "He used to tell me anything could happen in a poet's mind."

"Anything?" I say. The decorative brooch on her uniform today is a gold-plated conch shell.

"He could be in bed with me," she says, "and all of a sudden his point of view could jump to the North Pole or my mother before I was born"—she pauses—"or even some other girl. And those things would sneak in right under our covers."

My heart swells. I want to thank her. I look at you, I heave a sigh, I say, "I wonder where your point of view is now." She and I both giggle.

. . . .

But one day something starts to happen. The security guard comes downstairs again. He wants to move you again, I say no, Eva says come on, she escorts him out. I can't wait to rage with her about our tragedy-averted—but she doesn't return for three hours. I don't say anything about it. After that, her bathroom breaks get longer and longer. When I come back from my own breaks she is nowhere near you, sometimes a visitor is touching you on the bloodstain or photographing your crotch and I have to chase them away, she lets the baby's breath wilt in your pocket. I say he used to kiss with just the faintest teeth on my bottom lip, and she says really and I say don't you remember and she shrugs and touches the spot on her neck where little capillaries have been bursting lately like flowers. And then one morning she says I have an interview, I might be a docent in another room, the room with the bonsais—and that's the room the security guard is in, and she says, "Wish me luck," and she leaves.

And I am alone with you. For the first time in my life, I have you all the way. I shiver. I circle you like a prowling tiger for an hour before I close in enough to lean into your ear and tell you about her interview. But you don't say anything to make me feel better. I remember talking to Eva; she talked back. I look in your eyes stuck wide with death and I wonder what you would say to me if you were alive, and I know you aren't wondering what I would say to you. There is nothing I can do to make you wonder. Even after I have stabbed you. Even now. Your mind is yours, your heart is yours, I can kill you and keep you and chain you to the floor and still your point of view can be elsewhere.

It is one o'clock then two o'clock then close, and I am standing next to you and Eva doesn't come back. I guess she's gotten her promotion and now we won't eat lunch together anymore. What if the iron smell of you starts to smell like a stove pan instead of a warrior and I can't tell her. What if she gets a pretty new brooch and I don't know about it.

Something wet and heavy descends in my pelvis. Every part of me is crying. The Museum is empty; without knowing I'm about to do it, I grab my knife by the hilt and with one fluid yank I pull it out of your abdomen. The blade crumbles in my palm. You must have been acidic. I don't pause; I slide my hand into the hole beneath your navel. I bend my elbow, reach up, wriggle around. I wonder where your arteries are. I wonder how many periods I have left in me. I wonder if Eva is going to marry the security guard and forget about you and make babies and leave me to have you like you're not even worth having. I grab the stuff inside you. I feel what must be liver, what must be stomach, what must be spleen, all of it pliant and somehow familiar, the way when I used to fall asleep next to someone I would stop feeling where the two of us were touching because his flesh became the same as mine. And I push aside what must be lungs and then I hit something else: it feels like stone. It feels like something that never had blood in it. Instantly my hand recoils, back and out.

"Hey," I radio upstairs, "Eva, hey. Come feel this."

She comes. Her lips are blood-red with what she has been doing with the security guard. I pull her arm in through his torso next to mine, I guide her past the kidneys and intestines, up into the ribcage, I lead her to the threshold of the thing and then I stop. I wait for the shock on her face. Inside him I feel her reach it, the stone. She holds it. Her face doesn't change.

"What's wrong?" she says. She sounds annoyed that I have brought her down here over this.

"That thing," I say, but I am already suspecting, and now I wish she weren't here after all.

"The heart?" she says, and I know that I have never touched it before, his heart, and that she has cradled it in her palm so many times it feels the same to her as her own skin.

I can't look at her. "Go ahead," I say, my eyes on my shoes. "Go back upstairs."

She starts to. At the doorway, she turns. "Oh my sister," she says, and she runs back to me, and kisses me on the forehead, and then she leaves. I look at you. You are gaping empty above the belt. I have you but you won't kiss me. I grab at the stone, your heart. I hold it bloodless in my hand. My knuckles white with squeezing. Sometimes it seems impossible to feel un-sad.

FROM SOMEBODY
SO SCARED

. . . .

The girl I loved most out of anyone I've ever loved wants to come back to me.

This was the woman who, when we were supposed to be sleeping, instead I stayed up with my eyes wide memorizing how her hand looked blurred across my chest. This was the woman who, when she left me, I spent two days entirely in my too-hot bed. I didn't eat, I didn't sleep, I got up twice to pee, and I thought if I wasn't so possessed of the stupidest sliver of hope that she might turn back around, I'd open the window and move to the moon. This was the woman who, even now, half a lifetime later, to think of her is always physical. My stomach. My pelvis. My ribs.

She is standing on the front porch of my cabin. How many presidents have been sworn in and seen out since I knew her, and she doesn't even knock; she is leaning against the railing like she installed it herself.

"I'm sorry, K," she tells me. She sticks out a hapless hand, palm up. "It's raining."

I want to run a kitchen knife through her kidneys, but I am careful to light a cigarette instead. Of course it's raining. Her rusting bike is tied to a tree behind her. She is carrying a picnic basket draped in lace, I can smell maple syrup and see the thin hump of a record, and for this I could kill her and then I could kiss her and then I could kill her again.

"Bridget," I say. "You fucked up."

"I fucked up," she repeats, in the correct tone, not of contriteness or apology but of precision.

"I don't have a record player anymore," I say. Her hair is more gray than brown. My heart will fall out, I think. What will I do if my heart falls out. "I buried it with my father."

I am testing as I speak whether she still gives a shit. Instantly it's clear she does, she more than does, there is a waver to the way she holds the basket that almost makes me extend an arm to catch her.

I have hurt her, is what my brain thinks. Flat like that: I hurt her.

And then for the first time since I last woke to her hand between my thighs, pleasure lights my body like God stuck a finger through me, throat to floorboard.

"Come in," I say. She steps in off my front porch, remembering the dip that makes the entrance half an inch too low. She is thinner now except for her calves, she always had and will always have the fat calves of the potentially fat. I used to think, Good. More of her. I say, "Can I get you a drink?"

She looks across the living room, squints at the ice tray on my kitchen counter like she expects it to be spiked with arsenic. I laugh at her. All it takes is that hint of wariness and I know: she has gotten a fairytale of a life. Once upon a time when she knew me I was incapable of playing nice. Oh Bridget, I want to say. Only luck-loved bitches fail to understand how time can bend a person sideways.

I snuff my cigarette against the doorknob. She starts toward the kitchen, looks down, notices she is tracking mud on the hardwood that my dad replaced two summers after she left. She removes her shoes and leaves them neatly side-by-side at the front door, as if there are other phantom shoes she sees laid neatly side-by-side and not like wild lovers on their tongues. She sets the picnic basket on the counter.

"Blueberries," she says.

I am careful not to move my face into an expression whose mood she can read. I feel her watch me as I lift the lace off the basket and rearrange a glass bottle of orange juice and find the plastic box of berries.

I raise an eyebrow at her that means, Store-bought.

She laughs—the skin beside her eyes is wrinkled now—then something bursts through the middle of the laughter, and in the same subtle way that she used to transfigure sex to sleep she starts crying. She made the wrong choice, she tells me, where was her head, she's been so bored, so careful, she has missed her whole life. Every day of her life she has missed me, only she didn't see it until now. Now finally she has identified the absence gnawing under her breast. "It has a name," she says, and she looks at me under those wet lashes so long a scorpion could nest. The name she speaks is mine.

"So you christened the thing and now fuck it you're back," I say. I pop an ice cube, whole, into my mouth. Look, Bridget. I can be cold.

"I'm back," she agrees. Was she always my echo? I gesture frozen-tongued for her to sit somewhere, but I am still standing and she just leans on the counter. It's true that every other surface in the cabin is a mess, shirts and underwear and socks across the backs of chairs, ties I haven't worn in years, dresses because why not, scissors and glue and drawing pads, magazines, mousetraps, somewhere under the sink a rotting peach. She wipes her eyes. She says, "I'm going to convince you to keep me."

"You are doing it wrong," I say. I spill the orange juice down the sink and slide a bottle of Cabernet out from behind the toaster instead. I make sure she smiles; I wait to see it before I smile back. The rain beats on the roof. I edge the corkscrew into the cork. I am going to say no to her, but not just any no. I am going to say no to her in the way that hurts her most. I am going to find the way that will hurt her most and do it just like that.

………

Because the thing is, years ago she said no to me in the most painful way she could. She knew how it would ravage me and she did it anyway. I was young when it happened, though one toe was turning toward another and I plucked a gray hair every few weeks so I thought I was already old. I lived in this cabin in these woods and all I wanted was to not touch anything, because everybody was a stove and I couldn't learn; I always gave my hand. Yet I saw her through the window of the gallery where I'd been thinking of selling my work, and I walked inside. I knew by the speed with which she looked away from my lips that she'd never kissed a woman before. I thought: this one will be blank for me. I will be your wolf in the woods little girl, I will devour you. The only thing I will not do to you is lie.

Of course I kept a secret or two. I didn't say that losing the woman who'd left me before her had almost killed me, that after that woman I would stare at the mirror thinking what the hell is this body for, what is it for, tell me tell me, until my eyes blurred and I didn't look like me anymore and I asked my father whether the secret of the world was that everyone spent every night dreaming of their hands cupped open and nothing poured in. When I met Bridget, I told her everything except that girl. When Bridget got close to her, I snarled. I am vicious, I wanted her to understand. I am fanged. I used to think it was amazing that she didn't see: I am hurt, that's all.

But I don't think it's amazing anymore. A person who

has never been hurt cannot recognize pain's signposts. She leans on my counter with her smooth elbows and taps a fingernail on the wine bottle and says, "How have you been?"

"Great," I say, gesturing at the disaster of the living room, the bed so clearly trussed for one. There's a vibrator lying in plain sight on the pillow. "Really happy."

"I've been awful," she says, when I don't ask. I follow her eyes. She is not looking at the wreck of the floor or the bedsheets; she is scanning the walls, taking in the new collages in their frames. My old art project died years ago, I lost the ingenuity to make up poems for strangers. I started another project. Cut-out collages of a woman's slanted handwriting. There got to be so many that there's no wall anymore, just framed things I don't try to sell; I've been living, poorly, on the money my dad left me.

Bridget seems to be trying to read one of the fragments in a nearby frame. "I haven't had any passion, K," she says. "And just look at you."

I banish her to the living room. As if the thing I wanted was passion and nowhere to put it. The thing I wanted was power. I wanted choice. I wanted to make her knees lock when her feet tried walking away. An amateur astrologer once told me I had an inferno of a star chart, my sun in Leo, moon in Leo, Leo rising. Every house fire, the hottest chart she'd ever seen, I was deficient in water and air. I wanted water, Bridget. I didn't want passion. I wanted wanting, quenched.

She moves a loaf pan and an X-acto knife off the couch

and sits. She accepts a wine glass from my hand like a woman used to accepting glasses, not to climbing on the counter and opening the cabinet and rummaging around and having only herself to curse for not owning a single clean cup. A person who's never been hurt cannot recognize the tells in her body of having been loved.

"Bridget," I say, perching on the couch's arm. "How long have you been single?"

She says, "I'm married."

The diamond she is wearing sits atop her right-hand pinky finger. Such an easy trick.

I say, "To what?"

"A man," she says. I wait. "A man who's not happy but never complains. He's so staid, K. A fork of a man."

A fork of a man. Fuck her. She must have read a profile of my new work, a different kind of work these days than when she slept in my sheets, and she is quoting me.

I sip my wine with a show of slow savoring. I do not wipe the red remnants from my lips. I say the worst thing I can think of that isn't no. I say, "You are a bad writer."

She edges forward on her cushion, like we're staging a play together that's almost about to get good. She seems to take it as given that I have been reading her, too.

"You lie in your poetry now," I say. "You used to question yourself at least, *It isn't so bad to live / next door to yourself,* now all you write for is justification."

Back when I kissed her, I used to think she was the most beautiful poet. Heart-mangling, the way she broke a line, this ridiculous mystical who-gives-a-shit thing she could do, to put the right emphasis on the right word and crack the whole world open. So many times over the years I have glimpsed a thought of mine that seemed to have some truth I couldn't access nested underneath it; so many times I have needed my mind refracted through hers.

But her poems don't move me anymore. She has become trite, or stupid. Her adaptation, maybe, to a muted life.

"You've tried writing love," I say, "but you're not wise about love, Bridget. You've had so much of it." I have rehearsed these remarks in old imagined conversations with her. "It's made you gluttonous and unsharp in your seeing."

She seems to consider this. She squints one eye. Yes, maybe, she seems to say. Then she sets down her wine, stands, touches the glass over a cut-up near the foot of my bed. She says, "Your writing's different, too."

Well, you broke me, I almost answer. But I look at the cardboard box that sits at the foot of my bed, where I used to keep a record player. The box is labeled in my father's ugly scrawl. I know I must follow one principle, for this meeting I've dreamed of until the dreams grew nightmares: whatever Bridget wants, I will deny her.

I track her gaze. It glides off the wall, up my staircase, where beyond the loft I never enter anymore the town's rain-glazed steeple is just peaking through the window. She lets the silence sit. She has come back to beg me and here I am serving her drinks, and she's going to make me ask to hear her case.

So I will not ask. I open the box of blueberries on my lap. I take a small one between my teeth. It is ripe, firm and sweet and tangy; I make a show of spitting the mashed flesh out into my hand. I see on Bridget's face that this small rejection has stung her. Again that pleasure. I have not had pleasure in so long. I feel lush with it. I feel heat-seeking, coldblooded, vengeance-addled. I feel pleased that I am sitting down while she is standing up.

"When did I see you last?" I ask, though I know.

"The day I left," she says.

I nod. I add, "A Sunday." Can I shame her for not remembering the details. Will this be the sharpest way to deny her request to come back, will her own forgetting gut her.

"The seventeenth," she says.

I don't want the date to hurt. I want to be inured to it—I want all the earth's many revisitations to that particular position around the sun to have overwritten the only one that matters—but it strikes me like a hammer to the sternum.

"My worst September," I say.

She brings her gaze down, back into the living room with me. Oh Bridget, how I remember those black eyes, narrowed in exactly this way, when I used to say something you couldn't agree with.

"But we met in August," she says. Her eyes stay tight, confused. Perhaps she really has grown stupid. I can't tell what point she is trying to make, or else what prank she is trying to pull on me.

"We met in August," she repeats. "I left in January."

I shake my head. Could she be joking? What punchline could she possibly be winding up to? I reach behind the couch, past the clumps of hair and empty plastic water bottles, and unplug my phone from the outlet built into the floor. I open the calendar app and sneeze in the dust and scroll backward, empty years flashing under my thumb. And I show her: the seventeenth. A Sunday in September of that terrible year. In January, a Tuesday.

Her jaw falls slightly open. She sits back down on the couch. She shuts her eyes, counts something on her fingertips. I notice that I may be finding it by accident, the way to hurt her, to scramble her sense of what's possible until she doesn't recognize the clenched fist that has taken the place of her heart.

"You really don't remember," I say.

She shakes her head.

"When I tell the story," she says, "it was four months. August to January. We had a New Year's."

The rain has receded to an occasional fingernail-tap on the gutters. I notice, with some real animal fear, that her disorientation is making me feel scrambled, too. So much of the life we didn't have together would have been spent going over and over the story of the two of us. Honing it, reciting it for strangers, adding flourishes we both agreed to believe.

"So you've made your little adventure with a girl in the woods seem bigger," I say. "For the sake of the man in your bed. His sexy Bridget. The mouths of two women, the big round—"

"No."

I stop, not because of the word but because I can't remember if I've ever heard her speak it. She opens her eyes. She looks dead at me. "Six weeks was so much shorter than it really was," she says. She looks finally, pointedly, at the mess around us. "I hurt you worse than just six weeks."

"You left in September," I tell her. "I remember because the blackberries were in season."

A little "oh" sound, an intake of breath.

"September seventeenth," she says. "September. Six weeks was all we had."

....

My worst September morning: I remember what it looked like. She was leaving. The birds were singing something low and sad. My cabin had never had a mouse. My father was alive. He was walking through the orange-turning woods to bring me breakfast. I used to think, so often in the years after she left I used to think, what would have happened if she'd waited five more minutes? I wasn't good at keeping people. He was. He would have said Bridget, stay, calm down, let's talk. He would have shooed me to the bathroom, ignored the sex so lately in my hair, swept up the shattered frame splayed across the kitchen floor, put on a Coltrane, told a story about a younger, better me. The time I wheeled my mom around the house in a desk chair because her back was in spasm. The time I threw the spelling bee so my friend could win instead of me. Maybe he would have lied. Maybe he would have spun a myth for her about a day when I ran to the mailbox and he'd sent a postcard of a new star birthing silver in the sky. She would have stayed. He would have kept her, for me. I would have worshipped him for it. Bridget and I would own a house in western Mass with a trampoline and a tomato vine. Who knows. My dad could be alive. I could have kids who call him Pops.

"How did you handle it?" she says. "September eighteenth?"

"Well, Bridget," I say, "I'm alive."

"No," she says, again. She leans toward me on the armrest. She touches my knee, and it's fire. It's more than electric, I had forgotten, God used to sear me where she and I touched. I pull back. I knock the box of berries to the ground. "I want to know," Bridget says. "How? What did you do?"

I cross my leg over my knee. I have to quell that old instinct to tell her the truth: I don't know how I lived through it. Looking back I don't know how. I guess I slowly killed my father. I smashed everything in my cabin. I kicked the record player to springs and chips against the wall. I would go calm for weeks, manage to sell a piece of calligraphy or buy a tea at the diner in town. Then I would see a byline of hers in the publications I scoured, and I would know her poems were about me and then rage at their abstraction and then wonder if they weren't about me after all. I started hearing voices. I saw an angel on stilts walking over the treetops one early morning, I saw the way she split open her legs like I'd come right out of them. I called up to her. I set a trap for her. I tried to catch her like a squirrel in a loaf pan. I spoke to her and her friends, who knew me from other lifetimes. In other lives, they told me, Bridget and I had been together. In other lifetimes the roles were reversed, I was the one who didn't stick around. In other lifetimes I was a man and Bridget and I married and had children and I left her for a copper-eyed contortionist. In other lifetimes I was me and she was she and we lived right here in my cabin because she stayed. In future lifetimes, maybe. The angels weren't sure.

But then sometimes I would wake at night, alone and in a panic: we have not had other lifetimes together, Bridget and I, I would know this. I would call my father. This was the first time I've met her, I would tell him, and the only time I ever will. I would be smoking, madly. Drinking, madly. These were modes of survival but he didn't understand. He would come over and try to hide my cigarettes. He would tell me Kaye, move on, move on, there's a girl at the gym, at the grocery store, this one is somebody's daughter. Sometimes I would try to meet them. But by the time I arrived they'd have shifted the way the sun shifts between blinds; they'd have just met someone or been flirting with the woman ahead of me at the deli counter or been replaced a minute ago by the man who works nights. A life is decided by the buildup of such missed chances.

"I handled it as you'd expect," I say.

"You burned down Wineglorious," says Bridget.

She smiles. She thinks she can joke. She thinks she knows me. She thinks I am still such fire, she thinks she knows what she's returning to.

She doesn't know. Without her I have lived life waiting. Inside myself I've been a woman on her knees. My life has been a stall, not a life.

"No," I say. "I burned down Gallery."

She swallows. I can tell she's not sure if I'm lying, because what did happen to the gallery where she was working when we met was that it got broken into one Sunday and half the art stolen, I don't know by who; I was too busy screaming, calling 911, threatening to sue the world, because early that same morning my dad died.

My dad, my rat trapper, my breakfast bringer, my record singer, he had a heart attack in the cheese aisle and the butcher found him, still cradling a jar of my favorite marmalade. The voices I'd been speaking to shut up. He died and I inherited his stuff. In one box were the records he'd collected with me and my mom until I left for college, and in one box were the records he'd been planning to walk over to me every Sunday morning for the rest of our lives, and in one box were two hundred sealed letters from somebody so scared of going unanswered that she wrote her name twice on every envelope. *April,* said each letter. Front and back. I put on Patsy Cline on my computer. I sang along, my voice pitching high and then too constricted to come out.

I wanted to have been happy, before my father left me too. I wanted to have given him one image of me, happy. I opened a letter at random. Its contents made no sense. I opened another. Another.

And I learned: my dad had been married before my mom. He had woken in the middle of a cloudless night and rolled out of bed and walked barefoot out the door and not come back. His first wife, April, had been in the middle of loving him when he left. She had sent letters. Postmarked from southern Vermont, then northern Maine, then Nova Scotia. Year after year she licked glue that he never unsealed. She grew frenzied, sick, inhuman, she wrote that she felt like a piece of shit under his shoe, like a dog, like a demon, how could he ignore her and divorce her through the mail.

Each letter unopened. My beautiful father. Did he feel he was not responsible for her hurt? That it was best for her, somehow, to leave her cold?

I guess I am shivering on the arm of the couch. Bridget reaches for me again, for my hand this time, but she stops just short. She hovers over my skin, I can feel the low heat of her. Maybe I have made her scared to touch me. I hate that I can feel the familiar desire to hold her until her fear is gone.

"After the final no," she says.

"Wallace Stevens," I say. "Don't quote at me."

"Listen," she says. "I had to do what I did. I wish I didn't have to hurt you to get here, but there was no other way to become a woman who can say: I'm a rebellion now, K." The way she speaks my name. The consonant far in the dark of her throat. "I love you even when you won't let me."

Whatever thing in me that can still break is breaking. How dare she talk about her progress when I was its cost. I have not found a way to move forward. Or rather, I have moved forward, my heart has beaten, I'm older, my skin sags, but I have not found any way to be happy. The happiest I ever was, was with the astrologer in town just visiting. She had something of Bridget's smile and called me K instead of Kaye, I could hear the shortness on her tongue, and she was like a nicotine-patch version of Bridget. After her I cried for weeks when somewhere, elsewhere, Bridget wasn't crying.

Bridget's hand lands on mine, tentative as a butterfly. I let it stay. She leans forward. She takes my head, she tugs my neck, she kisses me. I don't have it within me to kiss back, I am short-circuiting. I hate you, I want to say. I love you, I want to say. There is nothing I can say to her: if I am sad it's not true enough, if I forgive her it's not true enough, if I miss her it's not true enough, if I could punch her it's not true enough, if I've grown or changed or moved on it's just as true as if I still feel exactly as I did on September 17 far too many earthly revolutions ago.

I break the kiss. "That absence with my name," I say. "Absences can't gnaw, you piece of shit."

This is my trump card. This is my way of saying, Bull shit, my love. You have never felt real absence in your life.

But Bridget doesn't concede. She says, "Mine does." She

says, "I have missed you, K. I don't expect you to think it's enough yet but I will stay until you do."

I look at her, too close to see clearly, this woman made of ice. She has a strength I don't have: my father's strength, to leave people behind.

"My answer's no," I say. "Get out."

She coils a strand of my hair around her finger. "I won't let you make me leave this time," she says.

"Bridget," I say. Maybe I am hissing. "I never made you do anything. Every choice you made, you made alone."

I feint as if to kiss her, but instead I bite her upper lip. I intend to draw blood. To my surprise, the edges of her lips curl upward. Did her husband teach her to like teeth, to crave some fervid brand of sex that I have been denied?

I slacken my bite. She moans. I listen, knowing that the game's not over, knowing with the certainty of a barefoot midnight leaver that I can sting her with waiting, but the time to maim her is when she thinks she has everything, when she thinks the danger has passed, when she thinks I will stay.

I let her pull me onto the couch. I let her start to undress me. I let her be amazed that I am wearing a long T-shirt, almost a dress, with only a pair of ratty underwear beneath. I don't make any attempts on her blouse. Her hands rush down my neck. She strokes the crescent moon tattooed on my chest like it's primordial, an ancient hieroglyph, the first thing she has ever touched. I remain patient as she moves past it, rediscovers my nipples, my navel, my hips. I wait for her to pull the snapped elastic aside and find my new tattoo, which is above my left-side pubic bone. It is a waxing gibbous moon, an almost-circle, the inverse of the crescent on my chest.

She finds it. I expect her to touch it, to kiss it, to trace it like a form of Braille—but she goes still. Something changes on her face.

"I wanted to have a different body," I say. "If you ever came back. I didn't want you to know me."

But Bridget doesn't seem to hear. She is rising to a crouch, then to her feet. Without removing her shirt or her bra or her ring she pulls off her jeans, yanking them, not loosening the button. I hear the zipper break. She pulls my head down in a motion much bolder than she used to be capable of, and displays her right-side pubic bone at my eye level, and I look.

She has a tattoo of a gibbous moon, too.

My heart almost stops. Something cosmic and tangled, an offering from whatever small human gods of light and refraction my angel used to speak to, I don't need to stack us to know that if we lay hip to hip our moons would align. I'd tried becoming my own perfect pair and all along Bridget was pairing me, miles away. And I am afraid, for the first time, that there is no way to hurt her so she ends up hurt worse than I do. If I send her away, then I will be alone again. I will have cut off my face to spite my face.

My brain isn't fast enough to change its plans. I say, "Bridget, I hate it. It doesn't mean a thing."

Conscious or not, she takes a half-step backward, toward the door. Only an hour and I've broken her resolve. Still I have a heart that doesn't work. A barrier of a heart. I look around me, at the left-behind woman's words that call my dad a knife, a fork, a spear. Bridget is standing in the middle of them, holding herself on the moon. The womb that neither of us ever used, the place I hold myself when I feel so big a loss inside so small a body I fear I will flip inside out.

There is no way to do it. I love her and so I cannot hurt her without hurting myself.

I rise to my knees. An animal skitters across the roof. We are face-to-face, her clothed above the hips, me below. "It's not fair of you," I say, "to come back to me. I have no choice."

"Then I will stay," she says.

I shake my head. I don't know how to say: Bridget. You have ruined me. The only way to make up for it is to have been ruined, too.

Because I can't say yes to her. If I take her fresh off someone else, then she will learn that someone else will take her fresh off me. She will never value our mutual yes as the lifeline on-your-knees impossible miraculous thing that it is. Because in Bridget's life, love isn't on-your-knees. Me, I'm a letter-writer with bruises on my shins. But Bridget has loved standing up.

"Sleep one thousand nights alone," I say. "Ache. That's my condition."

"But you'll sleep a thousand nights alone in the meantime," she says.

Time is cruel. Every second she spends without me is one I spend without her, too. I can't take companionship from her without giving it to her. I will always lap her in aloneness.

"So find me someone just like you," I say. "Get me a replacement. Then spend a thousand nights alone and then come back and see if maybe I still love you or if maybe you have lost me."

She is kissing my neck.

"I'm right here," she says, "right now. You can write a new story, K. Give yourself a happy ending. Sometimes there are those, too. Sometimes there are."

I want to believe her. Bridget, Bridget: my best gift, my sweetest dozens of days. The rustle of sheets when she first put her hand on my ribcage. All my dark-wood violin-mewling harvest-moon hopes. The rustle of couch now as she pulls my arm around her waist. The halting way I hold her, aware that she's been held. She maneuvers herself over me, straddles my newer moon, her hair swings in my mouth. "What are you thinking," she says. I can barely speak the words. She smiles. She says, "You feel lucky for once, my dour forest sprite?" I do. I kiss her. I think, so urgently I think, Kaye, let it be enough, such a gift does not come to everyone. Here it is, Kaye, all you've wanted, Bridget has come knocking at your door.

"My father used to say," I tell her, "that we are responsible for the things we've tamed."

"That's Antoine de Saint-Exupéry," she says.

"But then he wasn't."

She doesn't ask me what I mean. She says, "I bet he wished somebody else would be."

My father, I think. Here, for a moment, I give you the gift of my happiness. Take it. Examine it from every angle, peer between our lips and elbows, smile at my smile, put a record on some turntable of air, see how I grew up to be the image of the wife you left behind.

The sun slips through the slats between my blinds. The woman I have longed for stacks herself like one long galaxy on top of me.

"Bridget," I say. "I hope you know I'll never ever love you as I would have."

"I understand," she says. She laughs. "Just love me as you will."

MISSIVES

....

I got a phone call from my grandmother, who's dead.

"Nana?" I hoped. The night was so black I feared it would be my other grandmother, my mother's mother, who had grown up on the Upper East Side and spent my childhood telling me to keep my legs crossed like a lady.

"My darling Olivia," she said. "Why are you sleeping?"

Because it is dark and I have no one to stay awake for. I've given up my lists of men. The nights now are my own, no hand at my hip and no hip at my hand.

"Because I have been waiting for you to call."

"Wake up," said Nana. "Your cousin needs you."

I tried to think this mattered. During these long years alone, hoping Nana would reach down and pluck the right man from my endless lists, some moments have been sharp to me. Mostly dinners at the kitchen table with my parents. Sometimes my brother reading a book around his plate, though I've seen Isaac less on purpose, since his wedding. To which I brought no one. Tried to pick up a date among the groomsmen between dinner and dessert. When no one wanted me, I cried. My cousin Dinah pulled me to the bathroom, told me not to make a scene. Of course she wanted to scream, too, she said. But what if Nana was watching.

"Why does Dinah need me?"

Nana, I wanted to say. I'm the one who needs. Some moments since you've left me have been sharp to me. Most I don't remember and don't try. I fall asleep thinking I would rather be alive than dead, but I'd rather what's ahead than what has passed.

"Wake up, my Olivia," said Nana. "Your life is not a gift to sleep through. Even if it isn't what you'd wanted. Wake up and be in it."

"Dinah needs that man she loves," I said.

"She needs your looking-forward."

I don't have any. Nana. I couldn't bear to say goodbye to you. I couldn't look at your closed eyes. Why can't a lover call me from the past. Put one of them on, please. I can't keep losing. Not one more.

"You girls," said Nana. "My two girls. You don't want to see it: you are for each other."

....

I got a phone call from my grandmother, who's dead.

"Nana," I said. The night was as black as the gulf between my husband's thighs.

"My darling Isaac," she said. "Why are you smiling?"

Because my husband is asleep beside me. Because I still love him. Still, after all these years. Because he has been my life, has given me my life. Because God meant me to have no one and instead the ocean is crashing outside our doorstep.

"Because you are calling," I said. Because I have found a good life like you had with Pop, and I get to show you this life like a dinner I cooked on a plate.

"Don't smile," she told me. "Your cousin needs you."

My cousin Dinah. Dinah who has made a hard go harder. Am I my cousin's keeper, I thought of saying.

"You are your own keeper," said Nana. "She is her own keeper. But she needs a village. I am calling you."

I got a sudden horrible squeezing in my chest. My husband, I thought, and I reached for him, but it seemed he had gone from me. Nana, I thought, but aren't you proud of me? I have done everything I could, as much as I could. I have been good, I have been brave, I have loved fiercely. I have married. I have received bad prophecies and set them down. I have made good prophecies where I can. I would have opened that casket, if my sister and cousin had let me—I'd have been the last living eyes on you. I have tried as much as I can to be the women in our line of the lost, but I can't be. Nana, I have loved this lifetime. I have tried.

"But Nana," I said, "don't you have a message for me? For me, your only grandson, not for Dinah?"

Nana. I have wanted to be yours.

"Of course I do," she said, "my darling favorite. You are

a village. The student and the wise man both. Don't smile while your cousin cries. I'm calling you."

....

I got a phone call from my grandmother, who's dead.

"Nana?" I said. The night was so black, I couldn't tell the time. My heart was so black, I couldn't tell the year.

"My darling Dinah," she said. "Why aren't you laughing?"

Because he is gone. Our story is over, finally. I made him choose or I chose or no one chose, I can't remember, either way the man as I first loved him has disappeared. Maybe he took the me I was with him.

"Because you are gone," I said.

"My Dinah," said Nana, "but you are meant to laugh. You're so loved."

"But nothing's funny," I said. "Isaac and his husband rented a beach house. I saw it on Facebook. It has a fireplace and wine glasses that hang from a swing attached to the kitchen ceiling, and the photos they take are of each other."

Because I am sorry. Nana. I couldn't find a man who would make children with me; I never brought you a good life like dinner I cooked on a plate. I couldn't do it, Nana, though of all the people on earth I saw you last. In the back of a truck. Your body had crossed state lines and someone had to reconfirm. My father couldn't bear to look, my mother had to rub his shoulders, my cousin Olivia flat refused, my cousin Isaac thought it might be against our religion. So the responsibility fell to me. A truck driver opened the hatch. Then opened the casket. It was Nana, shrunken in a turquoise vest. To lose one person is to lose a world. I said, *That's her.* I didn't cry.

"What if no one else will ever love the fact that I sing them poop songs," I said. "A voice could sit inside me for the rest of my life, waiting to sing. No one will love that voice."

"Dinah," said Nana. "I have a message for your cousins, I have a message for my children, I have so much to say. But I called because the only message I have is for you."

My hope is dying. What will I do if my hope dies.

"Dinah," said Nana. "Life is so long. It is always too early to be sad, you hear? And it's never too late to be happy."

Nana who had lost her world.

Nana I have lost my world. Nana I'm not meant to be alone. Nana there is no one who will call me baby.

"So lose the world," she said. "So lose the world. Lose it over and over and over again. A new world always takes its place."

"A better world?" I said. "A worse world?"

"Lose them all," she said. "You are babybird in the palm of my hand in every one of them. There's nothing you've done wrong. A line that ends with you has simply reached its end. You contain all of us in that line of the living. Keep them. So lose the world. Keep us."

....

We got a phone call from our grandmother, who's dead.

"We did," says one cousin.

"We did," says another.

"Dinah," they say to me, "why are you crying?"

They've driven to my apartment; they climb into my bed. They stroke my hair with their pinky fingers. A lost world, a village, a brother and sister. The three of us, huddled bodies on the bed, alone.

You are everything, said Nana. You are all you need.

A NEW STORY

....

As you enter the second act of your life, you fall in love with a man who dreams of drowning. He grew up in a city below sea level, always threatening to pull him under.

"You are Jonah," you tell him. "Live inside me, I will be your whale."

You picture him a child, just a scared towheaded thing to pick up and tuck safe against your chest. You want to have been his mother. "I'm not Jonah then," he says. "I'm Oedipus." He laughs, pulling a strand of your black hair out of his mouth and crooking it behind your ear. You laugh, too. "Sure," you say, "Oedipus, why not, start off where I want you ending up, inside me always."

At night you dream of film noirs and Westerns, swashbucklers and epics. Cowboys cock their guns and pirates aim their cannons, but you raise him safe above the fray. He dreams of undertows that drag him low. He wakes up gasping, clinging to your waist; you rock him into you and tell him, "Breathe, hold on."

And then the flood comes bursting through your front door, and you can't save him after all. Your lover is no Jonah, you no whale. He tries to cling to you and drowns.

You picture it sometimes from God's perspective: your whole life just a circle of yellow hair sucked out the door-frame, spiraling downward, getting smaller. From the perspective of the ocean floor: your pinprick love appears, framed blurry-black against the sun, then swells and sharpens.

You will not picture it from your perspective: thrashing, bubbling, your front door bobbing past, why couldn't he swim baby why can't you swim you grew up underwater kick your legs rise up rise up rise up.

Your heart, gurgling.

After that, you start to dream of drowning. You are pressed against the ceiling in a flooded basement, but the plaster always cracks. The oceans overtop their shorelines, but you live somewhere landlocked, Kansas or Nebraska. He never shows up with you in these dreams. You wake and walk out to the coast, climb the fence around the rocks, wade in and hold your breath and try to drown. Underwater, you yell. *Come get me, come get me*, the call and response of it unanswered. His arm does not reach up to grab you. You bob to the surface. You cannot follow him; hair heavy on your neck, you know you have to leave this place. You leave. You move to an island in the middle of the Pacific. You learn the language. You let your hair grow long so it might catch on him and pull. You leap into the high tide during hurricanes, but all that happens is you get to be a stronger swimmer.

You begin to suspect: he couldn't have done it. Not if he is human in the same way you are. Your body is a buoy with airylight balloons for lungs. Either he is not a person, or you're not.

He is dead; you are lost; you can't tell which of you is more inhuman now. You go to churches, to drug dens, to psychic healers, to lucid dreamers. You meet a tailor with no thumbs. You meet a cellist with no ears. You begin to suspect: maybe you are always dreaming. One day you lock eyes with a shark. You think, *It's time*, you drop your head and expose your throat. It swims away.

That night, you cross the threshold of aloneness after which you feel eyes appear over your shoulder. That's when you figure it out. "Oh," you say to God, who must be listening. "He wasn't for this lifetime. In another century, I rescue him from a shipwreck and we raise a family in a cove. In the first millennium I was born out of his ribs, and in the second he survived the sea in mine."

"Wrong," says God. "The loss of him is not the kind of problem that you figure out."

Okay, fine, there is no figuring out. Only going deeper in. Floating above the thing or suffocating under it.

Or so God says.

You begin to suspect: this God of drowning is lying to you. You think you have his number now. Useless God. You stop frequenting the ocean. You leave your little island. You leave your things behind. Instead you wander deserts, sure now that you'll find him there, baking. What is the desert but the ocean floor, unmasked. He must have washed up somewhere in the Gobi.

For years you dig through sand dunes. You walk the yellow ground until your hair is blanched and your footprints lineless. Your calves grow hard. The only water you touch is in your canteen. Still you dream of drowning in it; still you drink the drops of what would drown you and survive. When asked, you say you're searching for your baby. You don't know who your helpers think you seek, son or lover; you tell them he clung to your chest.

It's possible some other things have loved you. It's possible you have been anchor to the man afraid of drifting. You have been wings to the man afraid of death by hanging, rope to the man afraid of falling off of edges.

It's possible you have been. You haven't noticed. You are wandering the ocean floor here in the sunlight, cacti in your sight, water at your hip, mouth wide open, sure you are a whale.

....

To miss him is like that, anyway. Something is wrong with the world: you aren't human or else he isn't; God isn't a god or else a god is nothing worth kneeling over; the ocean has no floor or else the floor is in the middle of the desert. The logic of the universe is skewed, two things cannot be true at once—that you could be his and he could be yours and yet the strongest thing you could assemble in your heart was not enough to make the thing inside his heart stay close to you.

....

Then suddenly it isn't like that anymore. How to account, in storytales, for the truth that love is nothing more than luck. Your naked body is a Chekhov's gun that never fires. Then one day and through no choice of your own, he reaches for the barrel. You aren't digging. You aren't praying. In all those lost years you weren't digging wrong, you weren't praying wrong. You do nothing more right or less wrong on the day you wake up in a dune and a pinprick in the distance, framed blurry-black against the sun, steps forward and resolves into his shape.

He is soaking. His hair is limp and matted, he is his own nightmares. What difference to you, by now, whether you're waking or dreaming; you press him to your chest.

"Look at you," you say. "Waterlogged. Don't worry, little sun, I've moved us to the desert, we'll dry you off."

You wrap him in a towel. You pluck the kelp from his teeth. The seaweed from between his toes. The barnacles from his white hair. You suck the water from his lungs, spit sea glass and pearls and eggs. "That's where you came from," you say, pointing to the eggs.

"Oedipus," he says, and laughs, and pulls a strand of your silver hair out of his mouth and tucks it behind your ear.

He remembers all your little fables since he's returned.

But now he studies your knuckles when he takes your hand. Your blue veins. *I've got you, I've got you*: the call and response of it, every night you practice, rocking like a ship, echolocating inside each other. He is tired-boned this time around, but still you love him with the force of wanting to be his mother. You are silver-haired this time around, but still you welcome him inside you and he comes. You say to God: If I am in a dream, then may I drown here.

Of course you cannot trust that trickster, God of drowning. He heard you or didn't hear you, either way there's something underwater about your love that you can't dry off. His forehead shines with salt. You wrap him in your arms, yet he shivers and shakes. You can tell: you are going to lose him again. Again the only word you will remember how to speak is *no*.

"There's nothing wrong with your arms," he says. "I'm only older now, and cold."

"But you went away," you say.

He tells you, "But I'm back."

You tell yourself it's true, the ways of love and life are random and inexplicable, sometimes he drowns in the sheets beside you and sometimes he resurfaces in the middle of the desert. But it's deep night, the hours where you lived while he was gone-away, and the things you know but cannot feel have no currency here. "Where were you all this time?" you say.

He doesn't know, or won't tell you. "God has given us a gift," he says. "Please take it."

"You're mad I didn't save you," you say.

He shakes his head. "You spent a lifetime teaching your-self a sorrowstory where I drowned and you couldn't. I was a person but you were a whale." He kisses your knuckles. "You were the person all along. You were breathing and I couldn't, for a long time."

He presses his lips to your neck, suction-tight. He shows you he can breathe.

....

This is the story I want to tell. The one where many years pass in the desert, because he doesn't leave, because of no because. Because he doesn't. No metaphor is truer than the fact of his body in your bed, day after day. After the years have gone, you're petting him one night when you forget why you are out here in the desert. His skin is salty and re-minds you pleasantly of the shore. You say, "Remind me, why are we so landlocked?"

He can't recall. He faces homeward. But the day you're meant to follow him, your body starts walking away. Can-teen bouncing at your hip, you find yourself bent over dig-ging through the sand. When he asks what you're doing, you say what even you are baffled by: you're searching for your baby. He takes your hand. He swears to you: you've found him.

So the two of you move home. The ocean crashes at your doorstep but isn't welcome and does not come in. You wake in deep night from your own dreams, of sharks with no eyes and gods with no teeth. But then you live on past the hour and he is here and gasping, reaching for your waist, having dreamed again of drowning.

For the rest of the life you share together, your dreams seem to know more than you do. In them, you picture it from God's perspective. You don't know why he went away, why he came back, who took him and what it was in the millennia he carries in his heart that returned him to you, but your toothless God knows: his towhead just a circle of white hair like a coin tossed in the ocean, now you see him, now you don't, a joke to play on reckless gamblers betting with their lives. From the perspective of the ocean floor: his body unwelcome, belched back up, told this is not the home he thinks it is.

From your perspective: so you missed the decades when he wasn't tired-boned. So you aren't a young mother or young lover, never have been, in your ancient dreams you were a thousand years old by the time you met him and even so you held him to your chest.

Finally in your dreams you picture it from his perspective: thrashing, gasping, wanting every day to breathe as you already could. Intending, all along, to make it back to you and stay.

....

Believe, believe, believe.

for the real Itta

ACKNOWLEDGMENTS

....

Having a book in the world was a long time coming. I am grateful first and above all to Sarah Munroe for picking this one out. I know that many wonderful manuscripts never make it into print; I've read too many of them. Thank you for being my good luck.

Thanks to Derek Krissoff, Sara Georgi, and the whole team at West Virginia University Press. Thank you to Gillian MacKenzie and Kate Johnson.

To my parents, Bernard and Phyllis Sender—I promise the next book will be dedicated to you! Thank you Dad for reading every story I have ever written, and Mom for always thinking I have something to say on the important subjects. And to my sister Hanna and brother Jeremy: May we always watch bad TV and talk about it like it's good. Thank you to all of you for being readers.

Thank you to the friends who have pushed me to keep on as a writer: Naomi Kanakia, who has kept me going in this field through all these years; Samo Gale, the best cheerleader any girl could ask for; Austin Allen; Dan Hornsby. Thank you to readers of this manuscript: Courtney Cox, brilliant and intuitive reader without whom I never would have finished this thing in the home stretch; Kate McQuade, Becky Hagenston, Seth Brady Tucker. Thanks to Deesha Philyaw for calling to talk; you are a model literary citizen, and I hope to pay it forward.

To the talented Amber Burke, Callie Siskel, Stacy Mattingly, Amanda Gunn, Arianne de Govia, David Weinstein, Kate Crosby: I can't wait to see your books in the world.

Thank you to the Johns Hopkins Writing Seminars for letting in this very young and naive girl and helping me to think of myself as a writer: Alice McDermott, Brad Leithauser, Jean McGarry, Mary Jo Salter, Matt Klam. Thank you to Justin Halberda for making me think bigger.

Thank you to James Arthur for first telling me about a thing called residencies, and to the residencies where my best creative work and happiest times as an adult have taken place: MacDowell, The Corporation of Yaddo, Ucross (and my wonderful cohort-mates there), the Virginia Center for the Creative Arts, Vermont Studio Center, the Atlantic Center for the Arts and Mitchell S. Jackson. Thank you to the George Bennett Fellowship at Phillips Exeter Academy, especially Todd Hearon. Thank you to the Greater Baltimore Cultural Alliance, to the Sewanee, Tin House, American Short Fiction, and Longleaf Writers' Conferences, and to TENT and Josh Lambert at the Yiddish Book Center.

Thank you to everyone at Harvard Divinity School: above all Kevin Madigan for the time and energy you have spent thinking through Holocaust literature with me; Stephanie Paulsell, Wendy McDowell, Terry Tempest Williams, Andrew Teeter, Matt Potts.

Thank you to my friends. I may have spent a long time unlucky in love—and you a long time hearing about it!—but I have been beyond the luckiest in friendship. So many of you offered reading and thinking-aloud and encouragement on previous books that never got picked up, but you deserve the thanks anyway:

My Baltimore family, roommates in at least three places with varying levels of infestation, who saw me working on this and many other manuscripts and helped me talk through them all: Samantha Hubbard, Darius Alix-Williams, Ashley Wilkes, Túlio Zille, Sabrina Bouarour, Luke Boardman, Julie Campbell. Cambridge friends: Meghan Finn, Juliana Cohen, Faith McClure, Christine Gross-Loh, Allison Gray, Paul Arsenault; and roommates who talked through and read various manuscripts: Karan Vansia, Eileen Enright, Edith Sangüeza, Marta Hodgkins-Sumner, Brady Bender. Exeter: Rohan Smith & Eva Gruesser, Mirella Gruesser-Smith, Nori Down, Chelsea Woodard, Mary Claire Nemeth. To my MFA cohort-mates Gwen Kirby, Eric Levitz, Jocelyn Slovak, Emily Parker, Alex Creighton, Richie Hofmann: Thank you for talking through writing with me at the early stages. To Scott

Snyder and Trouble for putting me on your fridge, Shira Concool, Jingying Yang, Dara Zyburo & Ben Margines & Derrick Ashong my pandemic medical consults, Laura Beavers for being my never-failing valentine and for sleeping two feet away from me; and to the friends who encouraged me in writing early on, Josh Silverstein, Diana Thiara, Jess Sturgill, Zai Divecha my fellow grammarian, David Lee, Amy Watson, Jeffrey Lazarus, Adi Elbaz, Eta Flamholz.

Debbie Hsu and Ellie Lipsky, you deserve your own category.

Gabriel Houck, for finally undoing some of my bad psychologizing.

Thank you to my Tufts and GrubStreet students; my Yale professors Courtney Zoffness, who first told me about MFAs, and Michael Cunningham and the late Sam See. Thanks to my wonderful teachers at Pascack Hills High School, who set me up to have a voice as well as anyone could: Debbie Brand, Virena Rossi, the late Nancy Harmon, Martin Shields, Doug Goodman, Dan Fallon; Rita Rome. To the Holland & Knight Holocaust Remembrance Project, Beth Am Temple, Rabbi Dan Pernick and in memory of Cantor Geri Zeller.

And thanks to my family: Aunt Jeannine and Uncle Fred, Danielle Dykeman & Greg Mogolesko and family, Aunt Adele Gold, TJ Dumser and the Dumser family, Mal & Sid Weiss, Rhonda Kogen, Judy Kessler, Rachel & Stacey Tepper. In honor of Nana Etty, and Grandma Shirley and

Pop-Pop. Mom and Dad, it's been a long list, and I'm putting you in twice to ensure Mom doesn't think she's chopped liver; thank you for always, unfailingly supporting me.

It has certainly taken a village.